PR

"...Michael Gear has transformed America's obsession with Hollywood beauty into an epic thriller of transcendent terror.

— JACK ANDERSON, PULITZER PRIZE-WINNING JOURNALIST

"Dr. Frankenstein has at last perfected his art and hung out his shingle in Hollywood...a hell of a novel."

— STEPHEN COONTS, *NEW YORK TIMES BESTSELLING AUTHOR*

"With a Crichton-like mix of scientific intrigue and pulse-pounding suspense, the Gears deliver a fascinating exploration of the frontiers of science."

— *BOOKLIST* ON *RAISING ABEL*

"Extraordinary .... Colorfully integrates authentic archaeological and anthropological details with a captivating story replete with romance, intrigue, mayhem, and a nail-biting climax."

— *LIBRARY JOURNAL* ON *PEOPLE OF THE OWL*

"Gripping plot, lots of action, well-developed characters, and a wealth of authentic historical facts."

—*BOOKLIST* ON *PEOPLE OF THE MASKS*

"Simple prose brightened by atmospheric detail sweeps this fluid, suspenseful mix of anthropological research and character-driven mystery to a solid, satisfying resolution."

—*PUBLISHERS WEEKLY* ON *PEOPLE OF THE MIST*

ATHENA'S WRATH

Also by W. Michael Gear

Big Horn Legacy

Dark Inheritance

The Foundation

Fracture Event

Long Ride Home

Raising Abel

Flight of the Hawk Series

The Moundville Duology

The Wyoming Chronicles

Saga of a Mountain Sage Series

The Anasazi Mysteries

The Athena Trilogy

ATHENA'S WRATH

THE ATHENA TRILOGY PART THREE

W. MICHAEL GEAR

Athena's Wrath
Paperback Edition

Wolfpack Publishing
701 S. Howard Ave. 106-324
Tampa, Florida 33609

wolfpackpublishing.com

This book is a work of fiction. Any references to historical events, real people or real places are used fictitiously. Other names, characters, places and events are products of the author's imagination, and any resemblance to actual events, places or persons, living or dead, is entirely coincidental.

Paperback ISBN 978-1-63977-183-7
eBook ISBN 978-1-63977-182-0

ATHENA'S WRATH

CHAPTER 1

So, this was what life in captivity was like? For Christal Anaya, being held prisoner aboard the renovated cruise ship *ZoeGen* could have been worse. Like, maybe a dark and dripping dungeon cell infested with rats instead of a Spartan cabin with a toilet and sink. Since the night Hank Abrams had abducted her from her apartment in Los Angeles, her life had really gone off the rails, and she was no closer to figuring out how the hell she was going to escape.

Unless she could figure out how to manipulate the man who now sat across from her in the ship's mess.

Christal shoveled food into her mouth as she studied Gregor McEwan. Since taking up her regimen of strenuous exercising, her appetite had grown accordingly. With the revelations given her by her fellow captive, geneticist Brian Everly, her interest in McEwan had blossomed. McEwan ran the Genesis Athena labs aboard *ZoeGen*.

He had brought her to the cafeteria; apparently it was the dinner hour because most of the other tables were filled with casually garbed technicians. A group of neatly groomed young men talked and laughed in the back as they bent over one of those little games played with black and white marbles.

"I'm not sure that holding you is such a good idea," McEwan noted, a thoughtful expression on his angular face. "The cost of food alone is exorbitant."

"So, let me go," she countered as she raised a spoonful of bangers and mash.

"Not until we can come to some sort of agreement."

"You know Hank?"

"Who?"

"Hank Abrams. The guy who kidnapped me, along with April and Gretchen."

He grunted, nodding. "They're a different part of the team. They work for Neal Gray. He's in charge of obtaining the samples. Why?"

"Hank said they wanted to make a deal with me. Up to now, no one has given me an incentive. And, Greg, I've—"

"Gregor, please. Greg makes my teeth hurt."

"Gotcha. No dentist on board, huh?" Christal chewed and balanced her spoon. "As I was saying, Gregor, locking me up in that little room where I can only stare at the walls and a round hole of ocean isn't buttering me up. It's pissing me off even more than I was pissed off to start with."

"Christal, I'm sorry, but you're considered a security risk. Put yourself in our position; would you just let someone with your capabilities wander around loose? To get into what kind of mischief?"

She wiped her mouth with her napkin and attacked the slice of apple pie. A gleam of interest lay behind his eyes. She knew that look, had seen it in men's eyes since she'd turned twelve.

All right, she'd use any vulnerability she could. She smiled. "Gregor, the point I'm trying to make is that you're a piss-poor salesman. Sending Hank down to try and bargain didn't start you off on your best foot. Get my drift?"

He warmed to her smile. "Then, I'm to understand that you'd be reasonable?"

"Sure." Her fork clattered on the empty plate. The two bodyguards were watching from their seats down the table. "Look, I'm as reasonable as the next person. But let's lay out the way it is, all right?"

"I'm listening."

"You guys steal my client's DNA. April socks me in the gut. Then Gretchen whizzes a slug past my head. Hank and April drug and kidnap me and carry me off to the *ZoeGen,* where you lock me into a tiny cubicle—enforced solitary confinement, right?"

He gave a slight wince.

Christal pointed a finger at him. "Now I've got a shitload to explain to my boss. The LA police, the FBI, my family—everybody's alerted to my abduction. I can tell you my mother is absolutely frantic by now. In short, this Neal Gray fellow just made a major fuckup."

"I see your point."

"Do you?" Christal leaned back. "Gregor, let's say I want to play ball. Like I said, I'm reasonable. Not only that, I'm ex-FBI. I know the system. I know how deep you guys are in now. As I see it, you've got two choices."

He leaned forward, elbows on the table. "And they are?"

"One, you keep me bottled up in my little room

until the Sheik comes to check out his latest prize; then you wrap chain around my neck and throw me overboard to go sight-see on the *Titanic.* The problem with that is that Christal Anaya has vanished forever, and unlike your missing geneticists, I've got powerful friends with money who probably aren't going to let loose of this thing."

"And the second option?"

"We come to an agreement." She shrugged. "It'll cost you, but I can go back, assure everyone that I had to make a split-second business decision. That I'm sorry for upsetting people, but Genesis Athena made me an offer I couldn't refuse. I can turn the official wrath so that Lymon Bridges, my previous employer, takes most of the heat. I make amends with my family, buy mom a new car, and apologize for worrying her."

He narrowed his eyes. "Why would you do this?"

She chuckled, gesturing around. "For the same reason you did. Come on, Gregor, you were abducted in the beginning, weren't you?"

He sighed, giving in. "Aye. They came out of the mist one morning when I was dying of a hangover. I was terrified, hauled off at gunpoint, and drugged. Much as you were. It wasn't until I began to see what they were doing, realized the possibilities..."

His eyes had taken on a glow. "Christal, there's a bloody fortune to be made here! What the twentieth century was to technology, the twenty-first will be for biotech. Imagine being in on the ground floor of a company like General Electric or Microsoft. That's what Genesis Athena will be. But more, because today we're talking global, not just national."

"Okay, but I'm still a little hazy on how this all works."

He grinned arrogantly. "Think of it like this: We have over eight and half billion people in the world, but they're still people. They share the same common human desires for health, family, and security. People will *pay* to obtain those things."

"And Genesis Athena can guarantee security?"

"Maybe not complete security, but security from illness, from birth defects, augmented immune systems, resistance to certain diseases"—he grinned—"the return of a dead loved one."

She frowned at that.

"Oh, come on, Christal. Think about it. The greatest single tragedy in human history is that of the lost child—the young adult taken before their time. Society as a whole can bemoan the notion of cloning a dead infant. It's a different story when it's *your* infant, whom you loved and cherished, whom you would give your very life, your soul, to bring back."

"Maybe for some."

"Maybe for all, once the notion gets around." Gregor waved it away. "Part of the resistance to the idea of creating life out of someone's cellular DNA is that it's still too new, reeking of the impossible. Of black magic, if you will."

"And it's not?"

"Heavens, no!" Gregor leaned forward again. "We're not talking wacko Raelians here. It's the future, Christal. It's adaptive. Look ahead into the next hundred years. As the population continues to grow, life will become ever more competitive. We're nearing a cap on our global resources. Maximizing productivity, knowledge, and redistribution of resources is the key to long-term survival. I'm not just talking at the individual level, but at the corporate, governmental, national, and international levels. It's a matter of positioning, of pooling talent and employing it."

"To do what?"

"Let's say a country pours fifteen percent of its GDP into health services for the prevention of contagious diseases, for degenerative and metabolic disorders, treatment of alcoholism and genetic disorders, not to mention care for the aged and infirm. For the sake of argument, we'll give our government an annual budget of one hundred billion. That being the case, fifteen billion is going to health care."

"Uh-huh. So what can Genesis Athena do?"

"What if we could approach that government with a genetic screening program that would save them ten billion a year?"

Christal blinked. "You're joking!"

"Oh, granted, we can't do anything about traumatic injury. People will continue to fall off buildings, crash their cars, get in fights, and burn themselves. No, what we *can* eliminate are the contagious, metabolic, and degenerative diseases. Beat the next COVID before it spreads. How? By simple gene therapies, by rapid genotypic scanning of fetal tissue from amniotic fluid. What would the government of South Africa pay to stop HIV cold? We can do that for them."

"No way!"

"Way," Gregor said flatly. "And here it is: We've isolated the gene sequence on the ape chromosome that makes chimpanzees resistant to HIV. For roughly two billion, we can build the labs, equip them, and guarantee that no child born with that additional complex of ape genes will be HIV positive in South Africa again."

She stared at him. "You're serious."

"Very much so. And that's just the tip of the iceberg. You ever been to South Africa? Roughly a third of the population is HIV positive. Johannesburg will change your comprehension. On one side of the street, I've seen a thirty-story glass-and-steel skyscraper. It might have been transplanted from downtown London, Frankfurt, or Hong Kong. The parking lot is filled with Mercedes, BMWs, and shiny Lexus autos. Across the street—I kid you not—is a refugee camp filled with a thousand people living in cardboard, tin, and plastic tarp shanties. They bathe and drink in the same ditch they defecate in."

"Why?" Christal shook her head. "Why do they do it?"

"Because Africa is teetering on the verge of catastrophe. The ANC is corrupt. Today in South Africa, the First World exists in a patchwork crazy quilt with the Third, often only separated by a single boulevard. It has to be seen to be believed."

"And Genesis Athena can fix that?"

"We can help." Gregor tilted his head, inquisitive eyes on Christal's. "Let's go back to our hypothetical model. What could they do with another ten billion a year? Build infrastructure? Educate their people? Develop industries and train new workers? Perhaps put it into agricultural production to feed their people?"

"Let me get this straight. You're telling me that Genesis Athena is out to save the world? That all this"

—she waved around at the ship—"is part of a mission for mankind?"

Gregor stared thoughtfully at the table in front of him. "The brutal truth is that we're a business. We intend to make a profit. We're no different than a hospital, and in a sense, we offer the same services. Health in return for payment for services rendered."

"And the cloning?" Did she dare mention the things Brian had told her? No. Not until she understood the dynamics.

"That's what we call vanity, or luxury services." He searched her eyes intently. "Like I said, it's a business. We're in a race to utilize as many genotypes as we can. The same with the genes themselves, like the chimpanzee immune sequence I mentioned earlier. Meanwhile, we have people paying small fortunes to have us re-create a dead child. Or, better than that, a dream child. We've cashed checks for over ten million on Elvis alone."

Christal gaped. "Ten *million?* Just for Elvis? It's hard to comprehend."

"Imagine trying to explain automobiles and airplanes to someone in Victorian England in the 1890s. People would have thought you daft. In fact, they'd have looked much the way you do right now, Christal Anaya. They'd have had that same skeptical look in their eyes."

"Do you really think you can do this?"

"Aye." He smiled fondly. "That's why I went with Genesis Athena. In another fifty years, my name will be spoken alongside Bill Gates, Elon Musk, Thomas Edison, and Henry Ford. My processes will have banished HIV, multiple sclerosis, Huntington's chorea, cystic fibrosis, and even susceptibility to such common diseases as tuberculosis, rubella, influenza, and rhinoviruses. My replicative procedures will be the standard for millions who wish to duplicate themselves. Lass, it's going to revolutionize everything."

Christal sensed his vulnerability. "I want to see this."

"I beg your pardon?"

She waved around at the cafeteria. "I'm in a secure part of the ship, right?"

"To put it mildly, I think you'd be harder pressed to get into the White House than out of here."

"Then let me see. Let me meet people." She glared when he started to object, stating, "Gregor, *I mean it.* What if you're not just blowing smoke? What if it's really true, and you can do all these things?"

"It is."

"Then why can't I make my own decision if I want in or not?"

CHAPTER 2

Sheela sat across from Felix Baylor in her first-floor meeting room. Felix had served as her attorney for years. He was one of the few people that she instinctively trusted. He was in his sixties, now. And looked it. The polished wooden table was already littered with papers from Felix's open leather briefcase.

"Jesus," Sheela whispered as she leaned back in the chair and scanned one of the stapled sheets Felix had given her.

"That's just the tip of the iceberg." Felix's voice pinched. "As near as my people can determine, Genesis Athena has somewhere in the neighborhood of two point six billion in assets in their publicly held corporation. My guess is that many of the entities who are major shareholders have even deeper pockets."

"And this Sheik Amud Abdulla?"

"He's the public figure. There are others, Sheela, people back in the shadows. I can't even begin to guess at this point." He hesitated. "And I'm not sure I want to."

She looked up. "Excuse me?"

Felix fitted the tips of his fingers together. "You asked me to set up a hypothetical inquiry from Jennifer Weaver. I did that. There was no risk involved for either you or me. I don't want to dig any deeper. If I do, flags are going to go up."

"Meaning what?"

He shrugged, creasing his sleek silk suit. "I'm not sure myself. I can tell you, however, that after years in this business, I can sense trouble when I'm sniffing at its door. If I send my people to ferret out the big guns behind Genesis Athena, I don't think we're going to like the results."

Sheela sat back in her chair. "I've never seen you scared before."

Felix took a deep breath. "I've never tripped over anything like this before. A great deal of wealth from Saudi Arabia, Kuwait, Qatar, Iran, Italy, the US, Argentina, Peru, and Great Britain is involved here. Even one Texas billionaire with a really unsavory reputation when it comes to outside interference in his affairs."

Sheela laid the sheet on the table in front of her. "Thank you, Felix. I won't ask you to do more for the time being."

He gave her a sidelong glance. "It doesn't mean that we can't sue, Sheela. Given what I've discovered"—he gestured at the papers before her—"we can still file. Genesis Athena invaded your privacy, stole your DNA for profit. What they're doing is morally, ethically, and legally reprehensible."

"You just told me you wouldn't want to tangle with these people."

"That's in a different realm." Felix smiled warily. "If we file suit, it will be a matter of record in a court of law. That's according to the rules, if you will. Then, during discovery, we can drag out the other names. That, too, will be according to the rules. They won't mess with the judicial system because of the unwanted attention it will bring them."

"Such subtle nuances."

"That's law. But if we go that route, you had better be prepared to settle out of court with a literal mountain of nondisclosure forms. They're going to want to bind that settlement up in iron chains."

She picked up the report again, reading through the several pages. "So, this is really it?"

"That's it."

"Christal hit it on the head, didn't she?" Sheela tapped her fingers on the paper. "Jesus, Felix, they're selling my DNA." She glanced up. "Can they really do that? Technically, I mean. Implant little copies of me into some other woman's womb?"

"Apparently. Yeah, I guess. They've done it with sheep, cattle, cats, monkeys, and apes. They're working on bringing back mammoths. The popular story is that there are too many variables for reliable cloning of a human being. You remember the Clonaid thing with the Raelians? After that people said it was too dangerous, that too many unknowns made it unreliable."

"Unless Genesis Athena knows something the rest of the world doesn't."

His expression was serious. "Given the amount of money they seem to have poured into this, they could be light-years beyond the current state of knowledge in university labs."

"Thank you, Felix." She indicated the report. "If you could set this up so easily, anyone else could, too. I need to think for a while. I'll be in touch."

Felix nodded, stood, and began replacing papers into his briefcase. "Sheela, I think it would be a good idea to let Rex know what we've discovered."

She stared at the neat paragraphs on the report, her heart like lead in her chest. "I'll tell him when I think the time is right."

"As you wish, but I want you to know that in my professional—"

"Yes, yes, I know." She waved him away. "But I'll keep my own counsel on this. Thank you again, Felix."

She watched him snap his briefcase closed, nod, and walk to the door. Only after it had clicked shut did she reach for her telephone. "Keep the faith, Christal, wherever you are. You're going to be part of the settlement."

She dialed a 1-800 number and picked up one of the bound reports Felix had left behind. When the voice on the other end said, *"Genesis Athena. Melinda speaking. How may I help you?"*

Sheela answered, "My name is Jennifer Weaver. My case number is 94-4443."

"One moment, please." A pause. *"I see that you're interested in a procedure for a Sheela Marks's baby."*

"Yes. I'd like to book a procedure, please." She made a face. "I'm afraid time is something of a problem. Could we do this soon?"

CHAPTER 3

From the *ZoeGen's* high railing Hank watched the white launch approach the ship. The small boat bobbed on the North Atlantic's deep blue swells. It seemed like an eternity since he, himself, had been one of the baffled visitors. From his vantage point on the rail, Hank watched the people clamber down the ladder to the craft. One was a petite blonde woman wearing a white windbreaker and slim jeans. She looked slightly unnerved as she leaped into the rising and falling boat. One by one he watched, counting no less than thirty-one passengers. Assuming fifty thousand a day as an average, that was a 1.6-million-dollar boatload down there. And the launches arrived three times a day for delivery and pickup.

He raised his eyes, looking out to the west. The cool breeze was blowing into his face, carrying with it the smells of salt, sea, and far-off land. He squinted past the razor-sharp horizon. There, somewhere just beyond the curve of the Atlantic, lay Halifax, Nova Scotia.

April appeared wearing a white sweater and tight

jeans. The wind whipped her copper-colored hair over her square shoulders. She looked over the railing, catching sight of the blonde, and remarked, *"Cha-ching!* There's another big chunk of change into the till. I just hope she was one of mine."

"One of yours?"

"The embryo she was implanted with. If it was one of my recoveries—say, Talia Roberts or Sheela Marks— I'm a couple of thousand dollars richer."

"That's your royalty, right?"

"Right." April leaned her head back, breathing deeply through her nose. "Rumor is that we've got another three big-dollar clients down in the lab. All Canadians. One of them for a child replication. The other two are enhancement jobs for rich kids."

"An enhancement?"

"Something about changing one of the base pairs to modify a sugar molecule in the brain cells." April made a face. "I'm way out of my area of expertise, but I think it's supposed to make the brain grow larger. Our people are into things like that. Simple little changes that give cells a slightly higher performance."

"What if it backfires? I'm just starting to understand the risks involved in fooling with people's genetics."

"There's risk in everything, Hank. You didn't go into the FBI without accepting a little risk."

"No, I guess I didn't." He smiled at that. "Funny, isn't it? The last place I'd have thought I was going to end up was on a ship in the Atlantic, preparing to steal other people's DNA."

"You'll retire rich."

"If we don't get busted first."

"We have insurance in the form of a crack legal team. Sometime it'll happen. As inevitable as rain. Cost of doing business and all. When it does, keep your mouth shut, call our attorneys, and let them settle. We've got some of the biggest guns in the business."

"Assuming we can come to terms with Christal. Kidnapping isn't just trespass."

Neal's voice came from behind. "We're working on her. The head of our genetics department has been talking to her. He seems to think she's coming around." Neal stepped up and looked down just as the launch cast off. White foam boiled under the stern as the launch bucked into the waves and headed for the invisible western shore.

"What's the plan?" April asked. "Vacation's fine, but I'm not adding to my investment by sitting out here, pleasant though it might be."

Neal leaned forward, staring down at the swells that rose and lapped below. "There's a complication."

"Why don't I like the way you said that?" Hank asked, turning, crossing his arms.

"You remember that motorcycle when we grabbed Anaya?"

"Yeah. The one you knocked over. I think I told you at the time it was a dumb thing to do."

Neal turned, his blond hair flipping in the wind. A coldness lay behind his blue eyes. "Want to take a guess as to who was on that bike?"

"Donald Trump. But he's sure it's a conspiracy against him."

"Try Sheela Marks. The driver was her bodyguard. I think you made his acquaintance."

Hank made a face. "Neal, I want you to know right

off: The guy's trouble. He's not just some rent-a-cop. Neither is he the usual stupid no-neck muscle guy recruited from a gym. He's the real thing. Don't underestimate him."

Neal pursed his lips. April was watching him, a cool appraisal in her eyes.

"It gets worse," Neal added. "It seems there was a paparazzo with a camera. The guy got photos."

"Shit." Hank turned, slapped his palm on the rail, and glared out at the endless expanse of water. The sun was riding high, well into its summer path. A group of gulls wheeled and ducked, checking them out before following the deck aft.

"What does that mean?" April asked.

"It means that Neal fucked up," Hank muttered.

"Hey! Don't start pointing the finger at me!" Neal barked. "You were the one who coordinated that whole operation, remember?"

Hank raised a hand. "Stop it! We're in the shit, Neal. You're the one who walked over and knocked the bike over. Prior to that, everything was explainable. But I'm not going to get into a pissing contest." He turned, glaring alternately at Neal and April. "I've been down this road before, so believe me, let's admit that we had a screwup, deal with it as a team, and go about fixing the problem instead of cutting each other's throats."

Neal was still hot, his face red and angry. "Right, smart guy. You got any ideas?"

Hank bit his lip, avoided Neal's eyes, and gave April a slight wink. She seemed to be hanging all her hopes on that. After a moment, he said, "The key to this is Anaya."

"Yeah," Neal said roughly. "I say we go down, walk her up here, and let her see if she can swim home."

"An injection would be quicker," April added. "We could dissect her in one of the labs and drop the pieces overboard. If you'll recall, they found Nancy Hartlee and identified her."

"Whoa, Nelly!" Hank raised his hands. "Jesus! It's a miracle you people have made it this far. You're about to compound one crime with another? You guys aren't any smarter than the damn hick criminals I've spent half my life slapping cuffs on."

He had their attention now; even Neal was calming down. Hank smiled. "Look, the thing is, you can't let it escalate. You start to panic, and intelligence goes out the door so fast it sucks logic and sense right out behind it. No, what we have to do is handle Anaya. Buy her off, convert her, brainwash her, I don't care; but the fact is that you've got to get her back to Los Angeles with a story that the cops can believe."

Neal looked unconvinced. "A bullet to the brain—"

"Don't even think it," Hank growled. "From here on out, put that thought out of your mind. Banish it. Be smarter."

"Smart how?" April asked. The chill had sharpened her complexion.

"A thousand ways," Hank answered. "She came here doped to the gills; she could leave the same way." He snapped his fingers as he looked around the ship. "All right, just for example, what would happen if our Christal was found two weeks from now passed out on a street in Kingston, Jamaica? Let's say she was injected with cocaine and ecstasy and with a blood alcohol content of two-point-two so that when the cops dropped her at the hospital, her toxicology read like a junkie's dream recipe. Meanwhile, someone calls her mom in New Mexico asking if Christal's there. When mom says no, our caller says, 'Well, she ripped off two hundred bucks from me in Key West, and I ain't gonna forget it!' When mom asks who this is, our caller says, 'Hey, I just party with the lady in LA, you know?' And we hang up."

Neal had begun to smile. April had lowered her chin, complicated thoughts shuttling back and forth behind her gray eyes. She asked, "Do you think that would work?"

"With a little embellishing, yeah. I mean, we'll have to fine-tune it, but it's got all the right ingredients. If she wants to babble about a ship, the feds will think it was a regular cruise ship. They've got an excuse to think she wasn't kidnapped. Instead, she was doing drugs, went AWOL with partying friends, and came to in Jamaica or wherever the hell we leave her. End of story, and we all go back to work." Hank lifted an eyebrow. "We've got the resources, right?"

"Uh-huh," Neal agreed. "But what about Anaya? She was after Genesis Athena in the beginning. She's going to know when she sobers up and flushes out that she was set up."

"Let her." Hank shrugged. "Look, the lady's got a bad rep with the Bureau. They'll be glad to wash their hands of her. As to her boss, he's an arrogant prick. If it looks like he's going to be tarred by her actions, I think he'll fire her butt and make sure she stays a thousand miles from Sheela Marks. The LAPD is going to read the FBI report and figure that Anaya just wasted a pile of their precious time. Without resources, Christal can say anything she wants. Who's going to believe her? Her credibility, along with five bucks, will get her a cup of coffee at Denny's, and that's that."

April looked at Neal. "When can we do this?"

Neal shrugged. "That depends on whether the Sheik wants to make a special trip out to see her. For the present, as soon as we finish with the last Canadian, we're heading south again. Reservations has another sixty clients coming out of New York for procedures. Depending on what the Sheik wants to do, I'd say that we wait for another week, set up the arrangements, and initiate the plan. It will take a while to score the drugs, fine-tune the details, and figure out how to move Anaya from here to there. I'll want to talk to McEwan, make sure that what we sedate her with won't leave a fingerprint." He glanced at Hank. "Is this time-critical?"

Hank shrugged. "I can't say. Probably not. The longer they look until they find her, the more pissed at her they're going to be."

April laughed suddenly, causing Hank to ask, "What?"

"You're going to enjoy this, aren't you?"

"Hey," he told her. "Paybacks are a bitch."

CHAPTER 4

That night, Mozart's Symphony No. 40 was playing on the sound system in Felix Baylor's oak-paneled home office on the ground floor of his twelve-million-dollar mansion. The place perched high on the flank of the Santa Monica Mountains just off Canyon Drive. He sat behind his huge teak desk, a snifter of Camus Borderies XO to his right. He had his laptop open, a copy of a contract glowing on the screen. If he looked to his left he could see through the large picture window and down the brush-choked slope to the city. The lights twinkled and shimmered. And the Beverly Hilton was glowing near where Whittier merged with Wilshire. Across the room—flanked by floor-to-ceiling bookcases—a large red cordovan couch with carved armrests dominated the wall.

Returning his attention to the contract, he frowned as he studied one of the clauses covering AI residuals and bent to the keyboard, overstriking a series of Xs over the offending part. What the hell did the studio take him for? A brainless idiot? Leaving that wording would have let them weasel their way into several million skimmed from streaming views.

He reached for the cognac, lifted the crystal bulb, and sipped. The door clicked, and he looked up, irritated. "Becky, I've told you..."

Lymon Bridges came striding into the room followed by a burly man in his midthirties, black-haired, in a casual coat and tie. The stranger closed the door behind him, flipping the lock home as Lymon crossed the floor.

"What the hell?" Felix stood, glaring. "Get the *hell* out of my house! Damn you, Lymon, you don't just show up here without some sort of appointment! I don't give a foggy damn what you told Becky..."

Bridges stepped around the desk, caught Felix's arm, and twisted. Felix screamed as a spear of pain lanced through his shoulder. He bent, following Lymon's lead as the man bulled him across the room and stuffed him face-forward into the plush red-leather Spanish couch.

Stunned, half-panicked, Felix heard the second man say, "So this is how the other half lives? Nice office. From the thickness of the walls, I'd say pretty much soundproof, too. No one'll hear the screams."

"Where is she?" Lymon demanded, bending down to growl into Felix's ear. He added torsion to the strained arm, and Felix screamed into the leather.

"I want to know it all, Felix. Every last bit of it. *Where is she?"*

"What are you—" His whimper was stifled as Lymon jammed a hard hand behind his neck and pressed his face deeper into the suffocating leather. Felix flopped, trying to kick out with his legs, feeling his shoes slip across the waxed maple floor.

"Uh, boss, you might let him catch a breath," the accomplice said mildly. "If you suffocate him, it'll take hours to rummage through all of his papers to find the right notes."

"Right, Sid." Lymon let up, allowing Felix to turn his head far enough to gasp a quick breath.

Sid—looking big in the corner of Felix's vision—bent down to stare. The look of disdain in those hard brown eyes sent a shiver through the lawyer's soul. He might have been an insect—one with interesting wings, but an insect nevertheless.

"Where is she?" Lymon repeated, a bit more leniently this time. "Where did she go?"

"I can't tell you. Lawyer-client priv..." He ended in a scream as Lymon twisted him into the leather again.

"Felix, that doesn't help," Sid chastised from the side. "You don't want to piss Lymon off. I've seen him rip a guy's arm clean out of the socket when he gets really pissed. We had an Al Qaeda raghead one time that cried for a day and half before Lymon finally lost his temper and broke his neck." A pause. "You know, the CO was so torqued off we had to walk patrol for two weeks in the hills after that." His voice dropped. "Are you feeling careless yet, Lymon?"

"I just might be."

Sid added, "Felix, old friend...can I call you old friend? Maybe you'd better just tell Lymon what he wants to know. That way you avoid all the pain, the surgery, the pills, the time in physical therapy."

"Where is she?" Lymon hissed into Felix's ear.

"Lymon, you're making a terrible mistake," Felix managed to mutter against the leather. "I'll have you up on charges for..." Lymon pushed his face into the cushions and wrenched the arm. Leather stifled the scream.

"Felix," Lymon said softly, "I'll tell you this once. Whatever she's gotten herself into, she's not up to it. So, you're going to tell me what she's doing...where she's gone. I don't give a rat's ass about privilege, because if anything's happened to her, I'm going to break your silly little neck."

"I'd listen to him, boss," Sid added solicitously. "Lymon's the kind of guy who'll twist your head off, shit down your neck, and afterward he'll screw your head on backward just out of sheer cussedness."

"How'd you get in here?" Felix's stumbling mind tried to latch onto something, anything, to give him a lever on the way to recovery.

"Locks were a hobby of mine in the military," Sid answered. "Yours weren't very challenging."

"Felix? You going to tell?" Lymon added.

The last of Felix's resolve drained away. He went limp, tears of frustration beaded at the edge of his vision. "Genesis Athena. She's after them."

Lymon released his hold, grabbing Felix's collar and turning him so that he sat facing forward on the couch. Looking up into those eyes gave Felix's stomach a cramp. "She asked me to set up an account under the name Jennifer Weaver."

"After the character she played in *Joy's Girl*?"

"Yes." Felix closed his eyes, looking down at his

rumpled shirt. The fine silk suit coat still looked pristine.

"Where did she go?"

Felix shook his head. "I don't know. Honest, Lymon. She didn't tell me. She had me set up an account, obtain an ID, credit cards...hell, I built an entire identity for her. Driver's license, everything."

Lymon drove a fist into a hard palm. It sounded like an oak beam snapping. Felix flinched. "She's going to have your ass, Lymon. Just like I'm going to."

"I want the file. You've got a copy."

"At the office."

"Then we're going to the office."

Felix swallowed hard, his mouth dry. A terrible violence lay behind Lymon's eyes, a look he'd never seen there before. "Why are you *doing* this?"

"Because she's in way over her head." The faintest thaw hovered around Lymon's lips. "Bless her heart, she thinks she can do something about it. Maybe figure a way to get Christal back, but she's walking into a snake's den."

"She didn't want you to know," Felix added. "Not you, not Rex, not Tony, nobody."

"Yeah," Lymon muttered. "I figured that out. But for the fact that Tomaso loves the lady almost as much as I do, she might even have gotten away with it. She scared the shit out of him when she made him drive her to the airport in his little Toyota."

Felix raised a hand in defeat. "Let me up, Lymon. Don't hurt me again. It's in my computer. I'll print you a copy of everything I've got."

Lymon reached down, pulled him to his feet, holding him close so that he could stare into Felix's eyes. It sent a deeper chill down Felix's spine. "One last thing, Felix. What happened here tonight, it's between you and me. Alone. Do you understand?"

Felix nodded, averted his eyes, and almost stumbled as he walked toward his desk to retrieve the files.

CHAPTER 5

Lymon led the way up the back steps to his second-floor office. Sid's heavy feet thudded on the metal behind him. As Lymon fished for his key, he asked, "Are you sure you want to be part of this?"

Sid stopped on the next stair down, his round face illuminated by the yellow security light. The night was alive with the sound of traffic, distant sirens, and the hum of the building fans. In the parking lot below, Lymon's Jaguar gleamed in the light.

"Yeah. I helped get Christal into this mess."

Lymon turned, slid his key into the lock, and opened the door. He took a right, flipping on the light as he walked through the storeroom to the safe in the back corner. He heard Sid lock the outside door before following.

The dial turned as Lymon input the combination. "You're a government employee, Sid. A federal agent. If this gets sticky, you don't have the approval of your supervisor. They could get real nasty with you." He looked back as he turned the handle to undog the latches.

Sid had a pensive look. "Sometimes, Lymon, things just get out of hand. It's the LA Field Office's case, but this Genesis Athena thing, it's related to my stuff. I can feel it in my gut."

"You know what they do to agents who go out on a limb?"

"They whack it off just to see how far they fall." Sid rolled his lips over his teeth. "I don't have time to fill out the 302s and jump through the hoops. If this works out, I'll get a reprimand, but I'll still break the case." He grinned sheepishly. "Uh, if you'll recall, we've had reprimands before."

"The problem is, we've got to be right. You understand that, don't you? You break the rules and fuck up at the same time, they hammer your ass."

"If it gets that bad, I hear that there's some guy in California wants to offer me a job."

"I can't hire you if you really fuck up and they throw you in jail."

"Let's try not to fuck up that much, okay?"

Lymon turned his attention to the safe. A rack of six HK Compact .40-caliber pistols rested on the padded top shelf. Boxes of CorBon .40 S&W cartridges were stacked next to a collection of high-capacity magazines. The lower shelves were filled with files of confidential correspondence, several sacks of bundled bills, agreements, and official LBA documents. In the bottom rested a black plastic case secured with a combination lock. This, Lymon bent and retrieved.

Sid frowned. "Is that what I think it is?"

"Yep." Lymon turned, plucking two of the magazines from the shelf and dropping them into his pocket. He then added a box of .40-caliber ammunition and finally slipped one of the HK pistols into his coat pocket. Locking the safe door, he lifted the lid on a storage box by his feet and retrieved a shoulder holster before leading the way to the hall and on to his office.

Sid was eyeing the heavy black plastic case that hung from Lymon's right hand. "I'm not going to ask if you've got a Class Three license for that thing."

"I do. All nice and legal." Lymon walked into his office, flopped the heavy black case on the desk, and unloaded his pockets of pistol, mags, and ammo before sloughing his coat off. He slipped his arms through the holster straps, opened the box of ammunition, and began thumbing cartridges into a magazine.

"So," Sid asked, "what's the plan? You know, you're not walking onto any airplane with a holster rig and magazines, no matter what you're licensed for."

Lymon glanced up as he slipped a magazine into the HK, worked the slide, and dropped the mag to top it off. "She's traveling under the name Jennifer Weaver. We've got her account number at Genesis Athena. When I pushed the redial on her phone, I got Delta Airlines reservations. They confirmed she boarded the five-p.m. flight for New York. Work it out."

"We're going to New York?" Sid made a face as he studied the black case. "You're outfitting for an operation into the Biqa Valley, not the Big Apple. I don't want to be the one to rain on your parade, but you don't have any legal leg to stand on if they catch you there with a pistol and an MP5." He pointed to the black case. "Assuming, that is, that you can even get past TSA and the rest of airport security with that stuff."

Lymon's grizzled brows lifted. "Oh, ye of little faith." He slipped the loaded pistol into the holster riding under his left arm, flipped through his Rolodex, and began punching numbers on the desk phone. He smiled at Sid as he raised the receiver to his ear.

It rang three times before a familiar voice answered, *"Hi, you've reached Vol Aviation. Bernie here."*

"Bernie? It's Lymon Bridges," Lymon began. "We've got an emergency. How soon can we be in the air for New York?"

"An hour and a half," Bernie answered after a slight hesitation. *"Uh, where did you say we were going again?"*

"New Jersey, actually. Teterboro."

"Right. I'll get the flight plan filed...fuel the jet. How many people?"

"Two."

"Right. Any special considerations?"

"Nope."

"I'll be ready."

"See you then." Lymon hung up the phone, grinning at Sid. "Charter, my friend. It's expensive as all hell, no security hassles, and I can guarantee you, the food's better."

Sid cracked a smile for the first time. "I could get to like this. Assuming, that is, that we don't get our tits into one hell of a ringer."

"You've read the files." Lymon finished loading his second magazine and dropped it into the holster's magazine pouch. "We've got to get to that marina in Brooklyn. We'll find her there."

"You'd better hope."

"Yeah, well, if not—if they pick her up first—Verele's going to have a very bad day until he spills his guts about Genesis Athena."

CHAPTER 6

Sheela sat in seat 4A and stared vacantly out the plastic window. She had seen the Mississippi pass below before the overcast closed in over Illinois. Now as she looked down, it was to watch a blanket of fluffy moonlit clouds roll slowly under her high-flying 767. The novel she held remained unread. She'd picked it up at the newsstand—something about archaeology and Southwestern witchcraft. The subject had made her think of Christal, but try as she might, she couldn't keep her attention on the story.

To her consternation, the in-flight seat-back programming offered *Blood Rage.* She did everything she could to avoid seeing her image on the small screens at each of the other seats. Would anyone glance up from their little glowing screens, notice her, and begin pointing?

She reached up, absently fingering the brown wig she wore. It was a quality job, as good as money could buy—and God alone knew she'd had enough experience with the finest makeup artists in the world to know how to make a wig look real.

She fought the urge to get up and walk to the lavatory. She'd already been there twice to see that her brown contacts hadn't slipped, to check her makeup and ensure that she hadn't smudged the olive complexion she'd so laboriously applied.

She was Jennifer Weaver now, a desperate and lonely woman traveling cross-country to fulfill a fantasy.

Bullshit! With each passing minute, she was growing ever more frightened, wondering what passing insanity had driven her to attempt this foolishness.

I won't let you down, Christal.

The image of her father's bloated face floated in the back of her mind. It left a tightness around her heart.

She ran her fingers along the edges of the novel, looking at the stylized image of Kokopelli embossed on the foiled cover.

Where are you, Christal? What are you doing?

She closed her eyes, thinking back to Christal's self-assured smile that day. God, the woman had seemed invincible. But twenty-four hours later, she'd been spirited away to where? The nightmare fantasies kept spinning in Sheela's mind. They were filled with brutality and rape. In each, Christal suffered in filthy and degrading conditions.

"I'll make them give you back," she whispered under her breath.

A sudden image of Lymon levered its way into her wheeling thoughts. She could see his disapproving expression, trace the lines of worry that would be forming there in the next day or so when he finally discovered that she'd disappeared. He'd be frantic. They all would. But she could count on Felix to keep a lid on it. He'd make sure they didn't do anything silly, like report her as a missing person.

Not telling Lymon hurt the worst. But she'd make it up to him. In the end, they'd have their day. She'd go, find out about Genesis Athena, decline their service at the last moment, and pay them enough to make it all right. Then she'd have the inside story. From there, Felix and his minions could apply the screws and break the whole damn thing wide open.

She closed her eyes. For the first time in years, she was doing something. Not for others, but for herself. For Christal, who'd offered her friendship without strings. For the little babies who would be born of this malicious procedure. Yes, it was worth being frightened,

A person's DNA should be sacrosanct, private and personal. It was hers, as it was Talia's, and Manny's, and all the others. Intimately part of their lives and bodies and souls. Why had no one seen this coming? Why had Congress, in all of its hearings, with all of its expert testimony, not preempted this? Where the hell had the Solons been when the news percolated with stories of genetics?

Democrats and Republicans. All too busy cutting each other's throats and playing silly games of one-upmanship and gotcha instead of working for the country.

If only she weren't so scared. If the fear would just loosen from around her guts. Damn it, this wasn't a movie. This was for real, with people who'd dared to kidnap someone as tough as Christal Anaya from right under their noses.

Genesis Athena had no idea that Jennifer Weaver was anything but what she seemed. It would be the role of a lifetime—only no one would ever know.

No one but me—and after all, who the hell else is there in the end?

One by one she thumbed the pages of the novel, the words unseen on the pages as her jet whisked ever eastward.

CHAPTER 7

Christal reveled in her newfound freedom. Earlier that morning McEwan had shown her the length and breadth of her current universe. After seeing the security arrangements, she wondered why the hell they'd bothered to lock her into her cubicle in the first place.

Her world now consisted of a small segment of H Deck on the ship's port side. A series of cabins were inhabited by various staff, most of whom Gregor had introduced her to. Each had been pleasant, professional, and reserved. English was obviously their second language, and from their reaction to her, Christal could tell that outside of the same coloration and complexion, they were from different worlds.

She had played dumb when Gregor introduced her to Brian Everly. It was apparent from Brian's expression that he'd rather engage in an intimate relationship with cholera than be in the same room with the Scottish geneticist. Two points for Brian.

There was one way in, and one way out, and it

passed through a monitored "go, no-go" steel hatch. The thing had been modified like the common jail access where only one door could be opened at a time, and then only when a security officer pressed the right button. The hallways were studded with video cameras. She could now walk to the cafeteria, to a small home theater with a DVD collection of the latest movies, to a common lounge with its TV, comfortable chairs, pool table, and games. A compact but complete gym and the attached women's locker room with its attendant showers was also available for her use.

The security camera in the women's shower had caused her some concern. She had to assume that it worked and that some man was watching. Modesty won out. She glowered up at the camera, then down at the stained pits on her blue blouse. It wasn't like they'd brought a wardrobe for her. She had what she'd been wearing the night they'd kidnapped her.

After McEwan had left, she'd availed herself of the gym, pounding out her aggression on the weight machines and treadmill. Flushed and dehydrated, she walked out into the hallway. With the towel hung over her shoulders, she dabbed at the perspiration beading on her face and throat. Her muscles had a deliciously loose and warm feel, and she absently studied the hoses, cables, and pipes that ran along the companionway ceiling. Was there some way she could exploit them? How?

"Christal?" a familiar voice called. She turned to see Brian Everly stepping out of a cabin.

"Brian." She let her towel hang and held her hands up. "Look! I'm free! Ready to fly away just as soon as I can cut a hole through the hull."

"What have you been doing?"

"Exercising. I'm hot, sweaty, and smelly, but I refuse to use the women's shower with that damned TV camera staring down."

He glanced around. "They let you out?"

"Gregor unlocked my door." She stepped in beside him. "He thinks he's got a chance to convert me to the side of money, greed, and corruption. That or throw me over the side to the sharks." She motioned around. "Besides, I've been up and down the halls. I'm not seeing anything I can fashion into a clever tool to make an escape."

He chuckled. "Good on you. But believe me we've been at it for five years. If there were a way, we'd have found it. I'm off for the cafeteria. You up for a bite?"

"Sure. Uh, provided you can either sit upwind or don't mind the smell."

Something in his smile sent a tickle through her. "Oh, I think I can endure. You have a nice scent."

"Liar." She walked at his side, glancing at him. "So, for five years no one has broken out of here?"

"Nancy Hartlee. And look where that got her."

"What about McEwan?"

"What about him? He's one of *them*. He can come and go as he pleases."

"How does he motivate you? I mean, you and the rest, you could just sit down and say 'Up yours' and refuse to lift a finger. Go on strike, if you will."

He gave her a sympathetic glance. "Have you ever heard the name Albert Speer?"

"Who?"

"Nazi general. He was the genius who kept Hitler's war machine running through the last years of the war.

A brilliant and evil man. While the Allies bombed German industry into rubble, he decentralized it, moved it underground, and kept a couple of million slave laborers producing munitions and aircraft." He smiled sadly. "McEwan is that sort. Bloody fucking brilliant."

"You could sabotage things."

He gave her a thoughtful look. "What if you were given a choice? That you could work and produce, or be the subject of Ebola research?"

"No shit?"

"Speer had bad guys in uniforms walking up and down the factory floors. If his workers failed to meet their quota, they were shot in the head. On the *ZoeGen* there are other means, just as persuasive, at McEwan's disposal." Brian smiled sourly. "Nowadays there are few of us left. The recently nabbed people, like Mike Harris and the rest, are at the facility in Yemen. If we don't take the buyout, who knows what will happen to us. There are two schools of thought on the matter. One is that after they pay us a bloody small fortune and we sign their nondisclosure agreement, they really will let us go. The second is that it will be cheaper to simply give us a sedative and sink our weighted bodies into the Rockall Trough."

"The where?"

"A really deep hole in the middle of the Atlantic."

"Oh."

He held the door to the cafeteria for her. "But, moving on to more delightful conversation, tell me about yourself. How on earth did you get here?"

Christal nodded at some of the now-familiar Arab technicians who sat at the end of one of the tables, drinking coffee. "I was researching Genesis Athena for my employer. I got too close. That and I caught the Sheik's eye at a New York film premiere. But we've talked about that already. I'd rather hear about what you're doing."

She walked over and took a tray and silverware. As they went through the line, selecting items, she said, "I mean, I've come to understand the why of it. Billions of dollars can be made. Where there's money, there's a way. But, like, why kidnap you people? Why not just hire you?"

He piled mashed potatoes on his plate. "Because of the legalities. Oh, I don't just mean the work itself, but, well, take Nancy's nanoscalpel. The University of California at Davis had filed on the patent. By stealing Nancy, Genesis Athena got all the information on how to build one of their own. They now hold the patent on a machine far in advance of the UC Davis device. Nancy's technology, coupled with Gregor's work on maintaining cytoplasm integrity in the oocyte, gave them the technique. I had a patent pending on my procedure for introducing nuclear DNA from dead cells into living ones. Mitch Harvey had perfected the procedure for isolating and introducing spermatozoic phospholipase C into—"

"Huh?" She gave him an askance look as they carried their trays to a table. "Talk English, all right?"

He grinned as he sat. "It's been years since I've had to describe things to the uninitiated, so stop me if I get too technical."

"Count on it."

He made a sphere with his hands. "Think of a cell as a complex organism, which, in a sense, it is. It has a skin that surrounds it and the equivalency of organs—called organelles—functioning inside it. At the heart is the nucleus—the center, where the DNA is. That's like the central computer. The cell itself is filled with cytoplasm, the nutrient-rich fluid in which the organelles float...no, that's a bad analogy. Let's say it's a gel in which the organelles are both suspended and interconnected—a chemical mix that has a great deal to do with the health and well-being of the cell itself."

"Right, I remember most of this from my biology class. But why was floating such a bad analogy?"

"Because in the beginning we didn't have any idea how important or intricate the cytoplasmic structure was when we were sucking nuclear DNA out of one cell and squirting it into another. It would be like sucking your heart out with a giant vacuum cleaner and blowing it into another person's chest. Think you'd survive the surgery?"

"God, no!"

"Right. You want to know why it took thousands of attempts to create Dolly way back in the nineties? It's because we didn't understand that we had to *carefully* extract the DNA without altering the delicate balance between the cytoplasm and organelles."

"You know, for years I've been losing sleep over that very question," she told him dryly.

He managed a grin. "It turns out that a cell is a lot like a factory. Raw materials go in; finished products and wastes come out. When we were sucking the nucleus out with a micropipette, it was like tearing out the head office with bulldozers. We were ruining the assembly lines, spilling product and goods here and there, pushing the machinery this way and that, and ripping great gaping holes in the factory wall. McEwan —bushranger that he is—was the first to figure out how critical the systemic organization and structure of the cytoplasm and organelles was. Nancy Hartlee, way across the world in California, devised her nanoscalpel, which allowed us to make an incision in the plasma membrane, the vitelline space, and the zona pellucida."

At her look of incomprehension, he added, "Those are the structures that make up the cellular wall of an oocyte—a human egg cell. Prior to that, we were literally crashing our way through the cell."

"Okay, I get the picture. By cutting you kept the shock to the egg cell down, right?"

"Right. Go back to the vacuum cleaner heart surgery we talked about. You want to traumatize the patient as little as possible. Cells, like animals, are tough and resistant, but they can only deal with so much trauma."

"You've covered McEwan and Hartlee. What was your contribution?" She thought his accent was musical and exotic.

He cut a piece of steak, saying, "I was the team leader on the first successful re-creation of an extinct species. You remember the Tasmanian wolves?"

"Yes! And the research leader disappeared. That was you?"

He made a mock bow. "At your service. Granted, we were still using the old shotgun approach, but we'd discovered that light and temperature affected cellular reproduction."

"Huh?"

He studied her over a forked broccoli. "Where does conception take place?"

"Well, as I understand it, in the fallopian tubes between the ovaries and uterus."

"Right, and tell me, Christal Anaya, how many fluorescent lights do you have in your fallopian tubes?"

"None of your business."

"Do you keep them at room temperature, or do you set your reproductive thermostat to body normal?"

"That depends on the man I'm with. For some, I keep it ice cold."

"And the others?"

"That's on a need-to-know basis, and as of now, you don't need to know." To change the subject, she said, "Okay, I get it. It's warm and dark inside."

"Brilliant! You've just hit on my part of the miracle. You see, cells are alive. They react to stimuli. My team proved that exposure to light changed a cell's function. Caused it to react differently."

He took a moment to eat his broccoli.

Oddly disturbed by the recent sexual banter, Christal studied him. Despite his current circumstance, some internal spirit buoyed him. He looked fit, and she couldn't help but notice the kindness behind his pale blue eyes.

"The thing you must understand," he began, "is that cells have complicated metabolisms. Just like the organs in your body, each organelle in a cell serves a particular function. The DNA is something like the brain and blueprint. It carries the instructions for operation. Surrounding it is the endoplasmic reticulum—the factory floor, if you will—where the cell builds proteins and synthesizes lipids, uh, the fats. The plasma membrane is the skin. Structures called mitochondria produce the energy, while the ribosomes manufacture various proteins the cell is tasked to make. Golgi bodies process and sort lipids as well as synthesize polysaccharides—a sort of structural sugar molecule."

"I didn't realize it was that complicated."

"Believe me, we're just scratching the surface of the structural components. We haven't even started with the intricate and delicate system of intracellular chemistry. It was there that my team made their contribution to the cloning of the Tasmanian wolves."

"I should have known."

"Don't be an irritant, Christal. It ill behooves a woman of your beauty and grace."

She was trying to decide how to respond when he continued with, "Light, you see, is energy. Plants, after all, live off it. While animal cells don't have chloroplasts—the organelles that handle photosynthesis in plant cells—why should we have been surprised that bright laboratory light, especially fluorescent light that pulses, affected discrete functions in the organelles?"

"So, you did it in the dark?"

"Right." He shrugged. "Couple that with McEwan's work, Nancy's nanoscalpel, and Harvey's PLCs—"

"Whoa! PLCs?"

"Phospholipase C s. The small case 's' stands for spermatozoa. If you'll recall, the last time I mentioned that, I got a similar perplexed look from you. You should look that way more often. It gives you a vulnerable quality that balances the normal man-killer fire in your eyes."

She started at the tone; his light jest masked deeper things. She remembered the look in his eyes that day when he'd first walked into her cabin: awe mixed with appreciation. So, what did she think about that? "Why don't you get back to this prophylactic CS."

"Phospholipase, not prophylactic. Though in a sense you might say they are related. The latter can be obtained in a little packet from a men's room wall dispenser while—all things coming to their natural conclusion—the former eventually ends up inside that selfsame latex."

He was playing with her, a twinkle in his eyes. Her confusion over the subject and her reaction to him just egged him on. To cover her fluster, she used a professional voice to ask, "Are you trying to make a point?"

"About PLCs? Yes. It's an enzyme, Christal. Mike Harris discovered that a very specific form of PLC is found only in spermatozoa."

"And why is that important?"

"Because it liberates calcium in the egg cell."

"I knew that. Eggs without calcium? The shells would be rubbery, and you couldn't crack them on a frying pan."

He ignored her. "In the simplest terms, PLCs tells the oocyte that it has been fertilized. It's a catalyst, a biological switch, one that releases a rush of calcium, which in turn tells a zygote—a fertilized egg—that it can start turning itself into an embryo."

He sipped at his coffee. "In the old days, we used electricity, and guess what? We didn't always get the result we wanted. Cells didn't like the electrical charge any more than you like putting your finger in a light socket. Harris's PLCs provided us with nature's much kinder and gentler key to boot the system."

"So, what you've been telling me is that you've

managed to fix most of the problems that caused clones to fail?"

"Welcome to Genesis Athena."

"Put this into perspective. Where are you compared to other labs?"

"Christal, we're light-years ahead. I've only given you a thumbnail sketch. Some of the applications are so technical you'd be lost by the descriptions of the chemistry alone. And then there's another whole universe in epigenetics."

"Epigenetics?"

"The nonprotein coding in DNA. We used to call it 'junk' DNA. Wait, let's go back. DNA codes for the production of different proteins, right?"

"Right."

"But if all the genes in your body worked twenty-four/seven, making all the proteins coded for in your DNA, there wouldn't be a difference between your liver and your big toe, would there?"

"I guess not."

"Each cell in your body carries your entire genetic code, be it an epithelial cheek cell, or a liver cell. So, what tells those cells how to be different? What to make? How much to make? And when to stop making it?"

"You wouldn't have brought up junk DNA unless the answer was there."

"Right. All those bits of old viral DNA, fossil genes, and apparent coding nonsense interact with signals from the cytoplasm to amplify or mute individual gene expression. This is done by something called methylation, literally tagging sections of DNA with methyl molecules that act as on-off switches. When something tampers with methylation in the noncoding DNA, the system goes haywire. It's the root of most cancers and all developmental and metabolic problems. We had to map and control the epigenetics before we could produce reliable clones."

"How does making a clone flip the wrong switches?"

"Individual cells react to trauma just like organisms do. In the early days when we removed or inserted nuclear DNA, the cell's cytoplasm and organelles were traumatized. They sent enzyme signals to the nucleus that popped methyl off entire gene sequences as the cell sought to repair itself. Think of thousands of switches being thrown randomly, lights going on and off, systems powering up and shutting down. We had to catalog the methyl tags before we could understand what we were doing to the oocyte."

"How many of these methyl tags have you found?"

"Over twenty million. And with them, we are closing in on the cure for most cancers. That alone will make the Sheik the richest man on earth."

"So, what's your success rate with clones?"

"Close to one hundred percent."

"Come on, conception doesn't even come close to that when it's left to nature."

All traces of humor left his face when he told her, "Nature is random, full of error and chance. With our control of epigenetics, we are slowly and surely removing those variables from the system."

"You're telling me that you can control the human genome?"

"Genesis Athena is about control, Christal. And don't you ever forget it."

CHAPTER 8

The woman had called from the Hilton's lobby. She would be knocking on the hotel room door within minutes.

Sheela took a deep breath, nerving herself, falling into her character. She was Jennifer Weaver, thirty-two, daughter of a once domineering and now very dead father and an overindulgent mother who had overdosed herself with sleeping pills when Jennifer was twelve. She knew this role, had played it so well years before that it had catapulted her into fame and fortune.

She had chosen a suite at the New York Hilton for her visit. The room had a view of the facing buildings on 54th Street, and by craning her neck she could just see traffic clogging Avenue of the Americas. She would have preferred the Plaza, or the Four Seasons, but even disguised, she feared that someone would recognize her. No, better to play it safe here, where she'd never stayed before.

The rapping at the door was professionally brief. Sheela stepped across, opened the door, and looked uncertainly at the woman who stood there. She wore a neat gray wool suit with a mid-length skirt, white conservative blouse, and coat tailored to her full figure. She might have been forty, with a round face and brown hair tastefully curled. Black pumps shod her feet, and a large leather case hung from her left hand.

"Jennifer?" the woman asked hopefully.

"Yes?" Sheela smiled uneasily, barely meeting the woman's eyes.

"Hello, I'm Mary Abernathy with Genesis Athena. May I come in?" Her smile was warm and reassuring, perfectly matching the friendliness in her eyes. She stepped forward, offering her hand.

Sheela gave it a limp shake before retreating to the small couch.

Abernathy took the chair that made up one corner of the triangle created by the TV, chair, and couch. "Let me begin by telling you a little about myself. I'm a registered nurse working with Genesis Athena. I'm here to do a pre-interview to get an idea about your general health, take a few samples for tests, and determine what we need to do to make you happy. I'm also here to answer any questions that you have; so please, don't hesitate, no matter how personal. Everything that happens here today is completely and totally confidential."

Jennifer Weaver nodded, smiled shyly, and fidgeted with her hands. "Okay."

"All right, first, let's get some baseline information." Nurse Abernathy reached into her leather case and withdrew a clipboard. "Most of the information has already been provided by your law firm. You're thirty-two, single, and living alone in Los Angeles, correct?"

"Uh-huh."

"Are you taking any drugs? Anything? From aspirin to LSD—we have to know."

"No. I've got aspirin and antihistamines in my purse. But I'm not on any prescription."

"No marijuana, cocaine, opioids, meth, or anything like that?"

"No." She shrugged. "Not recently. I mean in the last year or so. I'm clean. You'd find it in the blood test if I lied."

"Have you ever been pregnant before?"

Jennifer Weaver hesitated.

"It's all right," Abernathy confided, leaning forward over her clipboard, knowing eyes on Jennifer's. "By the time I was your age, I'd had a 'situation' myself."

"Yeah," Jennifer admitted, eyes downcast. "Once when I was fifteen, and again when I was nineteen."

"Did you abort or carry to term?"

"Abortion."

"At a regular clinic?"

"Yes. I had help. Daddy never knew." She sniffed angrily. "As if he'd given a damn."

Abernathy smiled sympathetically as she jotted something on her form. "What do fathers know, huh?" She looked up. "Tell me about your periods. Bad cramps?"

"No. Well...sometimes."

"How would you describe your flow? Heavy, medium, light?"

She shrugged. "Uh, medium, I guess."

"Any tenderness associated with either menses or ovulation?"

"A little, maybe. I don't know. I mean, I never take pills, or anything."

"Ever had STDs?"

"Yeah."

"When?"

"When I was younger. You know. I was a kid then. I didn't give a damn."

"What kind?"

"I had the clap when I was sixteen. Then a doctor told me I'd had chlamydia. He put me on pills for a couple of weeks."

"Did you take them all, or save some for later?"

"I took them all." She shook her head. "I didn't want the disease, you know? It's like being a whore or something when you've got disease."

"Well, before we do the procedure, we'll double-check and make sure everything's okay. Jennifer, have you had a pelvic exam recently?"

"Last November. Everything came back normal."

"Those times you were pregnant, how long did you wait before the abortion?"

She made a wincing face. "Four months with the first one. I was like really young, you know? I didn't know what to do. I was scared. The second time, I knew—I mean, I'd been through it before, so I only had that one for a little over a month. You know, just long enough that I knew I'd skipped. Then I got the test."

"No problems or complications?"

"No." She shrugged. "I didn't even bleed much afterward. I thought, you know, that I'd be laid up for days or something."

Abernathy smiled. "You look like a very fit young woman. How long since your last period? Can you give me a date?"

"Almost two weeks." She bit back any reaction as she thought of her stolen tampon.

Mary made the notation on her form. "So, you're almost ready to ovulate. Have you noticed any indication that you're close? Tenderness in the ovaries, vaginal discharge?"

"Not yet." She appeared to think. "But it should be soon."

"We might want to hurry you forward." Mary Abernathy looked up. "Outside of pregnancy, have you ever skipped periods?"

"Yeah, back when—" She looked away. "It was before Dad died. Before the trust was set up. He wanted to have me locked away. Sent off. Anywhere but where he was. You know. It wasn't a happy time in my life."

"So, it was stress related, you think?"

"Yes."

Abernathy didn't look up as she made notes on her form. "But nothing since?"

"No."

"I'm going to read off a list of diseases and health conditions. I need to know if you or anyone in your family has ever had any of these."

Through the long list that followed, Jennifer Weaver answered no to some, and yes to others, building the profile of her rich but unhappy life. Mary Abernathy dutifully noted each on her form.

Finally, she looked up. "Okay, Jennifer, that's it for the paperwork. Next, I need to do a quick physical. It's nothing to worry about." A smile. "I'll warm the stethoscope. The worst part is taking a routine blood sample for the lab. That will provide us with a baseline blood chemistry board, ensure that you're not having some problem, and confirm that your baby's immune system will be compatible with yours."

Jennifer swallowed. "Okay." She tried to look listless as Mary took her blood pressure, listened to her heart and lungs, but flinched when the blood sample was taken.

As Abernathy finished sealing and labeling her samples, she looked up. "Now, that wasn't so bad, was it?"

"No." Jennifer actually managed a weak smile.

"One last thing to do." Mary removed a plastic cup from her case, along with a plastic bag. Jennifer could see a Q-Tip inside. "I need you to walk back to the bathroom and give me a urine sample. Seal the cup when you're done. Finally, I want you to put your foot up on the toilet, just like inserting a tampon, and very carefully insert the Q-Tip and swab the inside of your vagina."

"Huh?" The request caught Sheela by surprise. She blinked the confusion away, pulled Jennifer's character back into place, and nodded reluctantly.

Mary Abernathy's expression turned serious. "If you'd like, I could help you."

"No." Jennifer stood, reaching for the cup and baggie. "That's all right. I think I've got the idea."

"Just be very careful not to contaminate either of them, okay? Don't lay the Q-Tip on the sink or toilet. Just drop it straight into the baggie when you're done and seal it."

As she went through the process, Sheela had to

wonder. Urine samples, well, sure. But the other? She made a face as she swabbed herself then dropped the Q-Tip into the baggie and sealed it.

Stepping out, she gave the samples to Abernathy and watched the woman write on them before she placed them in her case.

"Any questions?" Abernathy asked.

"Will it hurt?"

"The procedure? No." The nurse smiled. "You won't even know it happened."

"When will we do it?"

Abernathy shuffled through her papers. "If you're as close to ovulation as we think—and we'll know from hormone levels in the blood and urine samples—the sooner the better. Our lab ship, the *ZoeGen,* has just arrived off Long Island. I'm going to recommend that you leave as soon as possible. Can you do that? Go at a moment's notice?"

Jennifer nodded. "I'll be right here. Waiting, you know? I don't have any friends in New York."

At her expression, the nurse's professional demeanor seemed to crack the slightest bit, only to be replaced by the personable smile. "We'll be in touch, then."

"And the billing?" Jennifer asked. "That will all be handled through my attorney?"

"That's what I was told. Your deposit has been received, and your credit is approved. Provided that the tests don't indicate any problem, you'll be home in a week and pregnant with your new baby."

"It's that easy?"

The woman nodded. "It's that easy. We guarantee that your baby will be free of any genetic defects. But you are going to be warned so many times you'll have it memorized, so I'll start now: Jennifer, you must understand. We can't be responsible for what you do to yourself and your baby once you leave our facilities. Alcohol, tobacco, drugs, stimulants, certain foods, chemicals, poisons, and things like mercury that you introduce into your system can cause irreparable harm and are beyond our control."

"I know."

"Be sure that you do," Mary Abernathy told her firmly. "Jennifer, I'll be honest. We guarantee our work and the health of the fetus. We know our business well enough that we'll know if you cheat, understand? Our doctors will be giving you periodic checkups throughout your pregnancy. We are going to monitor both you and the baby very carefully. If you work with us and follow the rules, everything will end in a perfect delivery and a remarkable child."

"Will you be there?" Jennifer glanced away. "At the procedure, I mean?"

She nodded. "If you'd like. We're here for you, Jennifer. You're paying for the finest care and service on earth."

Jennifer looked uncertainly at Mary. "If...I mean..."

"Yes?"

In a small voice, she asked, "What if...if at the last minute, I change my mind?"

"It will be all right," Abernathy replied gently. "We'll deal with it when the time comes. This is a big decision. If you decide, for whatever reason, that you're uncomfortable, we'll call it off. No one will say anything. It's happened before. We want you happy so that when the time is right, you'll come back to us."

Sheela clenched her fist. "They said it would be a Sheela Marks's baby. That's what they promised. That's who my little girl will be, right?"

"Oh, yes," Nurse Abernathy answered. "We took her DNA right off of her tampon. Remember when that happened?"

"How could I forget?" she said too coldly.

CHAPTER 9

Rex sat fuming in Tony's plush reception area. ZTA, Zell Talent Agency, had its offices on the eighth and ninth floor of a high-rise off Melrose. A polished white marble floor gleamed under the lights, and the furniture was designer stuff Tony had picked up in London. A balcony hung over the waiting room where Rex fidgeted on one of the couches. Access to the sacred upper spaces where Tony hovered like God was gained by way of a sculpted staircase behind the reception desk.

Across from him, a woman in her forties, dressed in a brown Gucci concoction, held a huge brown leather purse in her lap while she consoled a pouting teenage boy dressed in baggy gray canvas. The kid had chunks of metal sticking out of his lips, nose, cheeks, and brows, as well as spiky black hair that stood out in all directions.

Rex shot a hard look at the receptionist, whose radar immediately picked up on it. She smiled, saying, "It will be just a moment longer, Mr. Gerber. Are you sure you wouldn't like anything? Coffee perhaps? Sparkling water?"

"I want Tony," he growled.

"Yo!" Tony called from above, his white leather shoes appearing on the steps as he descended and bent to peer down at Rex. "You've got him. Come on up, Rex."

"Hey!" the bratty teenager bitched. "I's here first, man."

Rex shot him the same sort of look he would have given an unwashed beggar pushing a grocery cart down Santa Monica Boulevard. The older woman was trying to hush the kid, hissing something about success and paying dues.

Rex flashed an empty smile at the receptionist as he hurried to the stairs and took them two at a time to Tony's upper level.

"I thought 'Yo' was out of style these days."

Tony grinned. "You never know. I might bring it back. So, Rex, what's up, babe? You look like, you know, bad shit's happening? I had to cut short a—"

"Can it," Rex muttered, leading the way down the hallway, past the assistants who watched from lowered eyes, past Tony's personal secretary, and into his large corner office. Rex made the 'close it' gesture with his finger, and Tony shut the door behind them.

"Sheela's missing." Rex stopped short, whirling, hands braced on his hips.

Tony stood with one hand on the doorknob, a confused look on his tanned face. Two thick gold chains could be seen behind the open throat of his shirt. "Missing?"

"Yeah, as in, I can't find her." Rex jabbed a finger at

Tony. "Tell me you've heard something. That she's called, left an email, messengered you, sent flowers, anything."

"Hey, man, the lady's been on my radar, but not since we had that meeting, you know? What's Lymon say?"

"The prick's gone, too. No one home. When I collared Tomaso—that Cuban dickhead that works for her—he just shrugged and said, 'Sheela left for a vacation.' End of story."

"A vacation?" Tony asked, amazed.

"Bullshit! It's all bullshit."

"What's Dot—"

"Nothing. She's still pissed about clearing Sheela's schedule. I called you about that, right?"

"Yeah, I got your message. I called Sheela's, but it was late. No answer." Tony looked up. "You're sure Dot doesn't know where she is?"

"Nope." Rex pursed his lips. "But I think Felix does."

Tony rubbed his face with a tanned hand as he walked over to the window that looked out toward the Hollywood Hills. "Give it a break, Rex. I think the lady pushed herself too hard."

"Excuse me?"

"She was burning out. Thing is, she was smart enough to see it coming. If you ask me, she's gone somewhere to lie on a beach without a phone, drink some good booze, and chill. You know what I mean?"

"If you'd let me finish, Felix knows something. I could hear it in his voice. When I asked about Lymon, he almost burst a vein. 'That son of a bitch! What did he tell you?' That's what Felix said, and he said it in a voice like I'd never heard him use before."

"I've heard you use that tone of voice before when Lymon's concerned."

"Genesis Athena," Rex stated bluntly.

"What?"

"The thing Christal Anaya was working on."

Tony smiled. "Yeah, Christal. They got any leads on her yet?"

"Nope." Rex paused. "What's that look for?"

"I'll never get to see if she was as good as she looked." Tony seemed to return to the conversation. "What about Genesis Athena?"

"I just came from Lymon's office. I said I needed to get in and find a file. That hyena woman that works for him was breathing over my shoulder the entire time to make sure that I didn't get into anything I shouldn't. When she started to get suspicious, I said that Lymon must have the file, and I'd get it from him."

"So where did Genesis Athena come from?"

"It was written on a notepad by Lymon's computer in big block letters, you know, like he was scratching it right through the paper. You know, the way people do when they're mad."

Tony frowned. "Wait a minute. You think that Sheela and Lymon are doing what? Chasing down Genesis Athena?"

Rex chewed his lip as he thought. "I don't know. But like I said, Felix does. When I mentioned Genesis Athena, he told me to go fuck myself."

"Felix said that?" Tony looked ever more thoughtful.

"Yeah. Not quite his style, huh?"

Tony placed a hand on Rex's shoulder. "Hey, you've been working too damn hard. Fuck it. If Sheela and

Lymon are out having a little tryst, more power to them, huh? You said that she practically admitted they were lovers that day at Lymon's. You're overreacting. Sheela wanted her calendar cleared so she and Lymon could disappear someplace where they could get it on in private. After what happened with de Giulio, I don't blame her."

Rex chewed harder on the inside of his lip, then shook his head. "I don't buy it. Sheela was pretty broken up about Anaya's kidnapping. She had that look. You know, the one that said she wasn't going to let it go."

"Fine, go wear yourself out, Rex." Tony walked to his desk, dropping into the easy chair. "Look, if the lady calls, I'll tell her you're worried. I promise, as soon as she hangs up, I'll use my caller ID to get the number, ring you, and you can get back to her. It's your funeral."

"Just hope it isn't hers, Tony."

He had already shrugged it off. "Only if the media gets hold of it. They'll have color photos of her and Lymon in flagrante around the world within minutes."

"So, you're going to do nothing?"

"Call me when you've really got something to worry about, Rex."

CHAPTER 10

The chatter of a helicopter beat its way through the *ZoeGen*'s maze of decks and companion ways. Christal blinked her eyes open, yawned, and stretched. She sat up on her hard bunk. Pale morning light was streaming in through the porthole. She threw off her blanket, stumbled over, and squinted out at the day. She could see the chopper, one of the fancy Sea Kings; it dropped out of the morning overcast, slowing. She lost it as it drifted out of her limited line of sight to settle on a helipad somewhere above. The chopper's whumpity-whump and whine died away to be replaced by the now-familiar ship's hum.

Christal rubbed her eyes and walked into her small bathroom. She used the toilet and splashed water on her face. She was feeling her damp shirt and pants—washed in her little sink the night before—when a knock came at her door.

"Just a minute!" she called, grabbing down her damp things. She whirled in anger when her door swung open. "Hey! I said, *just a minute*!"

To her surprise, Copperhead—dressed in a flattering pantsuit—stepped in and closed the cabin door behind her. She gave Christal a curious appraisal, noting the crumpled clothing Christal now held in a futile attempt at modesty.

"You look like a drowned rat," Copperhead stated frankly.

"Get the hell out of here!"

The woman smiled, hands loosely at her side, her weight perched on the balls of her feet. She wrinkled her nose. "Is that you, or is there something wrong with the plumbing?"

Christal's fingers cramped where they bunched her clothing. She considered flinging the whole mass at the woman as a distraction before she beat her to death.

"Go on," Copperhead said easily. "Get dressed. I'll meet you outside."

"Why?"

"You're wanted." With that, Copperhead laughed softly to herself, opened the door, and stepped out into the passageway.

Christal took a deep breath, shook her head, and began dressing. When she stepped out, Copperhead was leaning against the far wall, her arms crossed. She pushed off, looking Christal up and down. "Come on. This way." She started down the hallway. "We didn't think to bring you anything else to wear."

"Inconsiderate of you, don't you think, April?"

"If we ever do it again, we'll know."

"What? Kidnapping's not a normal activity?"

"Actually, you were my first. Change that. Let's say you were the first fully developed adult that I ever snatched. Some cells here and there don't count, right?" She gave her a wry smile. "Look, I'm sorry. Anaya, I don't have anything against you. Fact is, if you weren't good, we'd have never crossed swords in the first place."

"One of these days, I'm going to pay you back for those punches in the women's room. And I'm going to bust your dear little mousy Gretchen, too. I've never been shot at before—let alone with intent."

April took the turn that led to the only way out. "All I can tell you is that she won't be a problem in the future. She's been transferred."

"Oh? They had an opening at Gestapo charm school?"

"Tokyo. Among her several outstanding talents, she speaks both Japanese and Chinese. We project our Asian market to explode as Genesis Athena's capabilities become known. That's especially true of China and Japan where populations are plummeting. The point is, if you're gonna have a child, why not have exactly what you want? We'll make a fortune on little Xi Jinpings alone. Within twenty years, we expect it to be our largest market."

"Where are we going?" Christal asked as they approached the security door.

April entered a quick sequence on the keypad, leaned to look into a retinal scanner, then waved her wrist over it. She pressed her finger to the pad and addressed the camera, calling out, "It's the woman I told you about, Hans. Please pass us."

The door clicked, and Christal followed April into the small box. One wall was made up of thick glass, behind which sat a muscular blond man. Christal could see monitors off to either side displaying familiar images of the corridors, cafeteria, a laboratory, and the security door they'd just passed. He tapped instructions into a large control panel.

The outer door clicked, and April led the way into another of the ship's passageways.

"Was that the women's shower room I saw on one of his monitors?" Christal asked.

April nodded, indicating that Christal should precede her. "I hadn't thought of that. I suppose the others are so used to it they never give it a second thought anymore." A beat. "Hans and Max, who works the night shift, couldn't care less. They're lovers when they can manage to find the time."

Christal filed that away as she walked perhaps fifty steps and was directed to her right. "Take that first lift, if you will. Press the button for the B Deck."

When the doors opened, Christal stepped inside. Another of the ubiquitous security cameras glared down with a bulbous glass lens. She gestured toward it. "Doesn't that bother you? Being in the fisheye all the time?"

"We take security very seriously," April said as she stepped in across from Christal. "And if you're thinking of jumping me and making a break for it, we're about thirty miles offshore. If you're lucky, the water temperature is fifty degrees Fahrenheit. Instead of trying something that will end up making you look ridiculous, why don't you just cooperate for a while longer, and let the lawyers make their pitch."

Christal pressed the B button. "What's the pitch?"

"The cost of your current inconvenience and future silence."

"What if you can't afford it?"

The look April gave Christal was anything but reassuring. "Ms. Anaya, you're thirty miles out into the Atlantic. No one back on the mainland has the faintest idea of where you are. Hank says that you're a very bright woman, and my experience up to this point bears that out. We will be reasonable if you will. It's a simple equation."

The door slid open. Christal stepped out into a lavishly appointed corridor. The walls looked like they were done in hand-waxed teak. Golden sconces illuminated the rich carpeting and arched ceiling. The doors off to either side were wooden with gold handles. "Pretty chic," Christal muttered. "Is this part of the deal?"

"Just because circumstances put us on opposite sides doesn't mean it has to stay that way." April followed just behind her left shoulder. "Next door to the right."

Christal grabbed a slim handle, turned it, and stepped into what might have passed for a small lobby at a top-end hotel. Marble columns supported a sculptured ceiling. Gold filigree was everywhere. The floor was a combination of marble and sections of thick Persian rug. The furniture was immaculate, worth a fortune, and looked immanently comfortable.

"To your right. That door in the corner," April told her.

As Christal crossed the room, she looked out the tall windows that lined the far wall. Silver-blue ocean gleamed in the summer sunlight. Nothing marred the water's surface. Not a ship, not even a bit of flotsam.

The doorway led her into, of all things, a small

locker room with a tiled floor. On one wall, a redwood bench was backed by a full-length mirror. Floor-to-ceiling stainless steel lockers covered the other. Vanities filled the spaces to either side of the doors on either end of the room. They were accompanied by mirrors, hair dryers, and small sinks, all looking fully equipped.

April closed the door behind them. "If you'll remove your clothes and open that locker on the right, you'll see that we've taken the liberty of supplying you with a wardrobe. I think the size is right." She cocked her head. "Would you like to take a shower? One without a camera?"

Christal had taken up a position across from her. "What's up? Why are you doing this?"

"Some of our people would like to talk to you. We thought you might like to clean up and dress appropriately. You've got about an hour until they're scheduled to see you. If you want to go looking like you've just come off a two-week camping trip in the Guatemalan high country, who am I to complain? If not, there are clothes here and a shower room just beyond that door. You're welcome to clean up, wash, dry, and fix your hair. Whatever."

"And you?"

April pressed a key on the pad near the door they'd entered through. A solid-sounding click could be heard.

"I'm going for a swim." April bent her leg, slipped a shoe off, and began undressing. She looked at Christal with amusement as she peeled out of her pantsuit. "Like I said, we've got an hour. Use it anyway you'd like. Me, I'm taking it in the pool." She inclined her head toward the door at Christal's right.

Christal frowned, then opened it to see the sort of

shower a Roman emperor might have designed. The place was tiled in white marble with three sets of matching sculpted golden showerheads. When she looked back, April was naked, hanging her clothing in one of the lockers. The woman padded past on bare feet, walked calmly into the shower room, and turned on the water at one of the showers.

So, what are you going to do now?

Christal looked warily around the locker room, searching the corners for small cameras, microphones, or anything that might be suspicious. Back through the doorway, Christal could see April soaping her hair. If she was going to take her, now would be the time. Talk about vulnerability. Copperhead would never see her coming.

Her people want to talk to me?

She reached up to finger her stringy black hair. It felt tacky from the film left by the hand soap she used when she washed in her tiny cubicle sink. Then she glanced around at the opulent surroundings. Was this really legit?

What the hell.

Christal flipped out of her pumps and opened the locker April had indicated. Two white blouses, a gray wool skirt and jacket, and a neatly pressed pair of matching designer slacks hung there.

Maybe it wasn't the right decision, but she peeled out of her still-damp shirt and pants, laid them neatly on the redwood bench, undid her bra, and dropped her panties.

Vulnerable. Right. That's just how she felt as she walked through the door to the shower room. Damn! Talk about sybaritic! She hadn't seen that one full wall was mirrored. She took the faucet farthest from April, cranked the handles, and fiddled with the water until the temperature was right. The soap, shampoo, and conditioner were contained in gold-plated European-style dispensers with push buttons.

God, it felt heavenly. From under the spray, she watched April's reflection in the mirror as the muscular woman turned off the water, shook out her hair, and stepped to a far door. When April walked through, Christal could see the smooth turquoise surface of a pool under a glass-paned ceiling beyond.

Leaving the water running, Christal immediately slipped back into the locker room and tried the far door. Yep, locked all right. She returned to the shower room and turned off the water. Dripping her way to the pool room door, she opened it just a crack to peek out. April was churning her way through the water, stroking powerfully.

Christal glanced this way and that, seeing round life preservers here and there along the walls. Lounge chairs, small tables and benches, and several closed cabinets stood on the poolside patio. A diving board jutted out over the deep end closest to her.

"It's okay," April called where she trod water in the center of the pool. "We're not going to be disturbed. At least, not by anybody who will live through it if they do."

"Uh, I don't know."

"Suit yourself." April flipped over, diving like a dolphin, her feet rising from the water as she slid down to kick otterlike across the pool floor.

Christal could hear the voices, whispering, warning, as she glanced around, searching again for any sign of cameras, of observation.

Oh, do it! she chided herself. After all, April was buck-assed naked, and as she had pointed out, she wasn't the kind to take an infringement without serious consequences.

Christal stepped through the door, running to make a clean dive. As she speared into the water, a voice asked, *But what do you really know about her? This is Copperhead! Maybe she was a lap dancer at a strip club before she became a felon?*

Too late now. She was in the water. Her head broke the surface, and she flipped her wet hair aside.

April stroked past, floating on her back. "Feels good, doesn't it?"

"Whose place is this?" Christal found footing and braced herself, water modestly up to her neck.

"We have a lot of rich clients." April pulled her feet under her and stood in the chest-deep water. "That's why I brought you here. I thought you could use a break and some softening up before the lawyers get to you."

"Is that what this is, softening up?"

"Well, it's not a full-body massage, but it helps." April slicked the water from her face and pulled her wet hair back. She could have passed for Ursula Andress in *Doctor No.* "You want the truth?"

"Sure. Not that I'm betting I'll get it."

"Genesis Athena is a huge, bulky, and often unwieldy corporation. Sometimes management makes decisions that people in the field don't approve of. In your case, my bosses panicked. Hank didn't help matters any. He gave them a full report on you. Gretchen made a mess of the Manny de Clerk collection—and right after that, you walked into the answering service in Colorado. God knows how you put that together, but it blew everyone's minds. They had convinced themselves that you were going to be motoring up to the *ZoeGen* in a Zodiac boat and doing some sort of GI Jane commando raid by the next morning."

"Good idea. Anything explosive around here?"

"Just reality, Anaya. And sometimes that's more volatile than any chemical. Management didn't think that the public at large was ready for our reality to become common knowledge, and you might be the one to spill it. We want to introduce Genesis Athena in warm drips and drops, not scald the world with the whole giant corporate pot. We'll let people get used to the idea and then reveal a little more of our capability. By the time ten years have passed, people will be as comfortable with our abilities as they are with space flight."

Christal pushed off, sidestroking. April matched her pace. The woman seemed half porpoise. Where Christal had grown up, the deepest water was the chocolate-colored stuff that ran during the summer in the waist-deep acequia.

"What about the guys McEwan has locked up downstairs? They part of the business plan?"

"They'll be compensated."

"Uh-huh, how? Just like Nancy Hartlee?"

April pulled up, treading water in the deep end. "How did you hear about her?"

"Read the paper. The *New York Times* placed her story just under the fold. You know, wondering how she'd gotten from California five years ago to a watery grave off Long Island."

April jackknifed and dove; Christal splashed as she paddled around and started back for the shallow end.

April rose like Aphrodite in her path and sleeked her water-dark hair back with slim, shining hands. "You check the follow-up?"

"What do you mean?"

"About her family? The insurance?"

"Never heard of it."

"No, probably not. It didn't make the news that Nancy Hartlee had an unknown insurance policy. Assuming you decide to take our settlement, check it out when you get back." April pointed a hard finger, looking as dangerous as she ever had. "I know what you're thinking. No! We didn't drown her, throw her overboard, or anything else. It was her decision to go over the side. She was the one who tried to swim ashore. The miracle is that she made it as far as she did."

Christal stood, water coursing down her sides. "So what? I'm supposed to think Genesis Athena is run by a bunch of angels? Bullshit!"

"Angels? Not on your life, Anaya." April cocked her head, water running down her tanned skin and dripping from her breasts. "We're a business. An international corporation worth tens of billions that's struggling to be worth trillions. It's about global power and competition to be the world's foremost in biotech."

"And that justifies kidnapping? Stealing people's lives the way you stole Nancy Hartlee, Brian Everly, and the others? That gives you the right to humiliate Sheela Marks and terrify Manny de Clerk?"

"Look, I don't agree with everything they're doing. Just like I'm sure you didn't agree with everything the Bureau has done, is doing, or will do in the future. You've been around the block, Anaya. You're not some simple Pollyanna hick from New Mexico." She chuckled then as if laughing at herself. "Look, we're a lot alike, you and me."

"Don't count on it."

"Oh yeah? You were with the Bureau, one of their young hotshots. I was with LAPD. You got bounced by bad luck, coupled with a bit of bad timing."

"You seem to know a lot about me. Hank tell you all that?"

"My case is somewhat similar. I didn't get caught with my pants down. In my case, it turned out that my superiors were more interested in my body than my brains. With Genesis Athena, I can get as far as my wits and looks can take me." Challenge filled her eyes. "What about you, Christal?"

"What about me?"

"Genesis Athena could make you a very rich woman."

"As long as I didn't mind overlooking some things like kidnapping, extortion, theft, conspiracy, and a few niggling little ethical concerns?"

A faint smile graced April's perfect lips. "Nothing in life comes without compromise. But don't make that decision now. Take your time, hear what our people have to say. Then you need to think seriously about it."

"What, being bought off or dropped overboard?"

"We're not going to kill you." April leaned forward, stroking in a circle as Christal leaned back to float. "But you'd better know if you force us into it, we'll ruin you to protect ourselves. Paying you for your silence is the second option, but the first, the one we'd prefer, is that you consider a change in employment."

"Go to work for you?"

"Yeah. That's just what I'm saying. You're talented. You wouldn't have to do anything you didn't want to. Stealing DNA just happens to appeal to me personally, but we've got to provide security for clients, do research, lots of things that would suit your skills. I'm not trying to whitewash some of the things Genesis Athena does, but on the other hand, you could retire in twenty years with stock options and a couple of million in the bank."

"Just as long as I don't mind bending a few principles along the way."

April twisted in the water. "You'll bend them no matter what you choose concerning us. Life does that to people—forces them to compromise between Utopia and reality. I'm willing to bet your tax dollars go to fund programs and policies that you find ethically reprehensible, but I don't see you leaving the United States."

Christal slipped sideways into the water. "There's nothing I can do about what the government does with my tax dollars."

"Bullshit. You've just made that particular deal with the devil, Christal. You're comfortable with it. You get to live in familiar surroundings with certain services and protections, knowing at the same time that your government is buying off reptilian dictators, propping up sadistic governments, and hiding international murderers because they back us in the war on terrorism, or compromise drug rivals, or sell us cheap oil. Every day we make international criminals into millionaires and give them credibility—people that we'd arrest, convict, and lethally inject if they were on our streets. Or didn't you discover that during your days at the Bureau?"

"You're telling me it's the same thing with Genesis Athena?"

"Right down to the charity gene treatments we do for poor kids." April turned onto her back, spreading her arms, floating. "Genesis Athena is like your beloved American government—down to the last moral compromise. We do some bad things, some neutral deeds, and a lot of good stuff as well."

"Right."

"By the end of the next decade, no person on earth will have to be born with a genetic disease. That's forty million lives lived without mongolism, trisomy G, Huntington's, cystic fibrosis, Tay-Sachs, PKU, sickle cell, or thalassemia. No more ALS or muscular dystrophy."

"For a price."

"You ever been to the emergency room? There's always a price."

"I still don't think you're angels."

April kicked and regained her feet. "We're not." She waded close, where she could look into Christal's eyes. "But keep something in mind while you think about it: You're right. The cheapest thing would be for us to tie a chunk of metal around your ankle and drop you overboard, but you know what? We're not going to do that. We're offering to make amends, settle for the inconvenience."

"Why?"

"Because you've still got a surprise or two coming. Time's about up. You've got a meeting." April climbed out of the pool, striding for the shower room.

Christal flipped back her wet hair as she waded for the steps. She wiped water from her skin and stared thoughtfully at the wet footprints she followed.

A business. Did she believe that? That Genesis Athena was just a huge amoral Goliath crashing its way through people's lives?

April was already under the shower, rinsing the chlorine away. She turned her back to the spray as Christal walked in.

"Here's the deal, Anaya. Somewhere down the line Genesis Athena and its personnel will be held responsible for their actions. Time and money, along with charitable actions, can lessen the blow, dull the sharp tongue of censure, but we'll still have to face the music."

"Damn right." Crystal twisted the knobs and rinsed under the warm water. She felt truly clean for the first time in days.

April shut off her faucet, water trickling down her tanned skin. The beads of it glistened in the bright overhead lights. She stood defiantly, head back, her firm thighs slightly apart. "We're not fools. Everything that we're doing now will eventually come out. At least, that's how we have to plan for the future. Knowing that, it will serve us in the long run to make amends for our mistakes now."

Christal turned off the water and walked over to face her. "Is that what you told Nancy Hartlee? What about the other slaves you've got locked up down below?"

April stepped over and pressed a tile beside the mirrored wall.

Christal jumped as warm dry air began blowing out of slim vents artfully fitted between the sections of mirror. She braced herself, squinting into the warm rush. In awe, she watched her mirrored reflection. Her skin was moving as if under an invisible caress. As the jets changed, her breasts slowly lifted and rolled. The pressure sharpened her cheekbones, outlined her abs, and lifted her black hair. As it dried, it began to flow out behind her in a raven wave. She had never seen herself like this: a Native goddess, firm and slim, brown and muscular.

"Quite the thing, isn't it?" April asked beside her. "Lean into it. Shake your hair out. If you turn, it will slick the water away."

Eyes slitted against the wind, Christal studied the woman as she posed before the mirrors, her actions slow, graceful, almost like tai chi. Copperhead laughed aloud as the waves of air rolled over her body.

Christal tried to match her movements, turning slowly, trying to balance gracefully against the pushing air. It felt great. No wonder the rich lived like they did.

April touched the tile again; the warm air vanished as if but a memory. She was looking Christal up and down as if she were a prize racehorse rather than a security risk. A faint smile curled the woman's lips. "Bottom line: It's business. We'd prefer to fix the problem now rather than take the loss in the long run."

Christal walked into the locker room, gaze fixing dismally on her grungy clothes where they lay on the redwood bench.

"Put on the new ones." April might have been

reading her mind. "Leave those. I'll have them laundered and delivered to you later."

As Christal inspected the locker's contents, she found a new brassiere and panties, still in packaging. When she dressed in one of the new white blouses, she wasn't surprised to discover it was her size exactly.

Fix the problem? Take the loss in the long run? Just what, exactly, was Copperhead after?

"What would it take?" April asked as she hooked her bra clips. "Our terms, once you boil down all the bullshit lawyer talk, are that you drop any and all charges, that you sign a nondisclosure agreement, and that you never reveal any of the things you have learned here or elsewhere about Genesis Athena."

Christal considered for a moment and said, "Five million."

April laughed. "Not a chance."

"So, what's your counteroffer?"

"Two hundred thousand."

"What makes you think I wouldn't take it and spill my guts later anyway?"

April's gray gaze cut like diamond. "Because we're a business, Anaya. You have a basic understanding of our capabilities, resources, and resolve. I think you know that we'll use them if we have to. We'll keep our end of the bargain only as long as you keep yours."

"I'll think about it." Christal pulled the classy gray skirt up and zipped it. "Let's go have this meeting."

April worked her arms into her pantsuit and stopped long enough to pull a brush from one of the vanity drawers to brush her shoulder-length hair.

"You ready?"

"Yes."

April reached over and pressed the keypad on the door lock plate. She opened it and led the way out into the marble-columned lobby. Christal barely cleared the door before she came up short.

Sheik Amud Abdulla—backed by two sturdy-looking men—stood waiting for them. He was dressed in a sleek black silk suit and was smiling, a gleam in his dark-brown eyes. He nodded to April as though in satisfied approbation.

Christal's guts squirmed when the man turned his raptorial attention to her. He started with her feet, gaze slowly rising, savoring, as he took in her legs, the fitted skirt, white blouse, and tailored suit coat. Christal swallowed hard when he fixed on her face, a dreamy smile on his lips.

"Your meeting is canceled," the Sheik said in perfect English. "Miss Hayes, please take Miss Anaya back to her quarters. We wouldn't want to cause her fatigue in her current condition."

CHAPTER 11

June Rosen answered on the first ring: *"Lymon Bridges Associates. How may I help you?"*

Lymon leaned back behind the steering wheel in his rental car. He and Sid had picked a small commercial lot across the street from the Brooklyn charter boat service, paid the tire shop owner to let them sit and set up camp. "It's Lymon. I was just checking in. Anything happening I should know about?"

"The police called. They've still got nothing on Christal's disappearance. On the same subject, her mother called twice yesterday asking if there was news. Agent Harness' wife called—"

"Yeah, Sid checked in with Claire a little while ago." Lymon glanced across the seat and out the passenger window at the taunting gates of the charter service. "He's got his home fires covered, but his squad supervisor in Washington is starting to chafe at his continued use of personal time."

"And last, but definitely not least, Rex was here yester-

day. He insisted that you had a file of his on your desk. I took him back and watched him like a hawk to make sure he didn't get into anything."

"Was he a good boy?"

"For the most part. He seemed to fix on your notepad and frowned. You'd scribbled 'Genesis Athena' there."

Lymon considered that. "I think it's all right."

"Where are you?"

"Waiting in a parking lot across from the charter service in Brooklyn. We've seen people going in and out all morning, but none of them was Sheela. It's been long enough we're wondering if we made the right move."

"If you need moral support, call. In the meantime, I've got two new clients. I'm sending Salvatore as detail leader to cover one and Wu for the other."

"Good work, June. Do what you have to."

"You, too."

Lymon canceled the call just as Sid came walking up with a box of donuts and two cups of coffee in a carrier. He opened the passenger door and slipped into the seat. "Sorry, boss, but the only chocolate donuts had those little sprinkles on them, so that's what you got. But me, I got my crème-filled."

"Got the receipt?" Lymon asked as he took coffee and a donut.

Sid handed it over, and Lymon carefully noted the expense, folded it double, and placed it in his pocket. "Did you know that IRS stands for Invasive Rectal Service?"

Sid gave him a sidelong glance. "Huh?"

"You know, that feeling you get every April fifteenth when you bend over and spread."

"Do I detect a note of latent hostility?"

"You don't have to deal with the paperwork. Yet."

Sid sipped his coffee. "There you go again, trying to woo me away from serving my country with—Whoa! Cab pulling up."

"Yeah, I got it." Lymon reached for the binoculars and watched as a brown-haired woman in the back seat used her credit card to pay the driver. The trunk sprang open. Next the cabbie got out and walked around to remove a familiar suitcase. The woman had stepped out from behind the cab.

"It's her." Lymon snapped the binoculars down and shoved them into his pocket. "Brown wig and darker complexion, but I'd know that walk anywhere."

"Let's roll," Sid said as he popped the door open.

Lymon was already out, striding purposefully across the street. He could hear Sid's steps ringing on the pavement behind him.

A middle-aged woman they had watched arrive earlier stepped out of the covered walkway, smiling. Lymon was close enough to hear her say, "Jennifer! I'm so glad you made it! Any trouble?"

Jennifer? Was she still pretending to be Jennifer Weaver? Using the account Felix had told them about?

"No trouble," Sheela's voice answered as she faced the woman. But not Sheela's voice. She sounded somehow small, insecure.

"Excuse me!" Lymon called, quickening his step. He saw Sheela turn—recognized her face despite the brown hair, but the brown eyes would have fooled him. *Play along, Lymon, until you know what's coming down.*

Sheela gasped with recognition as Lymon said, "Jennifer? Can we have a word?"

The middle-aged woman stepped forward, a frown on her face. "Who are you?"

"Jennifer's security firm, ma'am." Lymon pointed to Sid. "This is Agent Harness, and I'm Detail Leader Bridges. Jennifer is our principal."

The woman was watching him with a hawklike intensity, trying to gauge his veracity. Sheela, on the other hand, looked like a spotlighted deer: anger, confusion, and disbelief all boiling under her pinched expression.

"Lymon," she finally hissed, "what *are* you doing here?"

He gave her a bluff smile. "Look, Jennifer, when you hired us, you hired the best. We're just doing what we're paid to do."

"Lymon!" she cried, trying to find the words. He could see the incipient panic on her face. Every instinct in his body and soul was to grab her, cover, and run.

"Jennifer, it's all right." He held his hands up. "You didn't hire us to make moral or ethical judgments on your life. We're not priests. We're protection. Period." He glanced at the middle-aged woman. "She's not doing anything illegal, is she?"

"What? No!" the woman cried. "Ms. Weaver is here on personal business."

"Then there's no call for alarm." Lymon shrugged. He recalled the character, saw the vampish insecurity she was projecting straight from her stellar on-screen performance in *Joy's Girl.*

"Lymon," Sheela growled. "I don't have time for this now! I have a boat to catch."

Lymon glanced at the other woman. She had her

arms crossed, clearly on the verge of calling for help. "How long are you going to be gone for?"

By now, Sheela was recovering. He'd seen that steely glint before, knew that hardening of the mouth. She was getting pissed. No way he'd be able to talk her out of this. Instead, he nodded at Sid. "Go get our bags."

"What?" Sheela cried.

"Ma'am, my job is your personal safety. If you have a problem with that, you can fire me right now. Right here." He hoped his eyes communicated his desperation as his stare bored into her brown contacts. "I don't know what you're into, but as your security, I advise against it."

She seemed to waver, on the verge of actually telling him to go to hell. "All right, Lymon. Come on." She turned. "There's lodging for them?"

The hard woman was watching him through eyes that would have burned holes in cement. "There will be an additional charge, Ms. Weaver, but yes."

"It's all right. I can pay." Arrogance was in Sheela's voice as she waved it off as a minor annoyance. She seemed to be firmly back in character.

Sid was already waddling back, various bags under both arms as he dodged a garbage truck that came barreling down the street.

Lymon gave a professional nod, wondering what the hell Sheela was doing. He was unable to read the emotion behind her dark-brown contacts. From the set of her mouth, however, he figured he was in for a real tongue-lashing when they finally had some privacy.

CHAPTER 12

Did she reach up, grab him by the throat, and choke the living daylights out of him, or did she throw her arms around him and kiss him full on the lips?

Sheela considered both options as she sat on the cushions inside the covered cabin on the forty-foot launch. She was one of sixteen passengers aboard. Lymon and Sid Harness leaned against the rail at the stern, no more than ten feet behind her. They might have been passengers on a pleasure cruise for all the concern they showed. Their luggage was piled next to hers on the deck.

On the right, across the murky water, the lower Manhattan skyline passed, and Long Island's blocky buildings crowded the shoreline to the left.

Among the other passengers were two very pregnant young women on the opposite bench. They acted as if they knew each other, but Sheela couldn't hear their conversation over the roar of the twin engines. In the front, a sickly-looking man who might have been in his midtwenties was traveling with a woman who seemed to be his nurse. A young couple sat immediately across from her—a man and his wife—both in their midtwenties. They had been introduced as Bill and Wyla Smith.

When Sheela had asked whose baby they were going to have, Wyla had replied, "Why, our own, of course. My father died of Huntington's, and I'm going to have it as well."

"How do you know?"

"Genetic screening. I have three too many trinucleotides on my fourth chromosome. Through Genesis Athena, Bill and I can make sure that our baby won't face my fate and my father's."

They went on, explaining about something called CAG nucleotide repeats that were completely beyond Sheela's comprehension. To cut the lecture short, she asked Wyla, "But you've already got it? Can't they do something about it? Cure it?"

Bill smiled at his wife and tightened his hold on her hand. "We've been talking to the people at Genesis Athena. They say they can cure it through a gene therapy they're working on. It's still experimental. For the time being, we can afford to have the baby fixed. We'll go back and treat Wyla when we can pay for the rest of the procedure." A pause. "And you, Ms. Weaver?"

She gave them an uncomfortable smile. "I'm having a Sheela Marks baby."

They gave her a blank look as if they didn't understand.

Sheela avoided their eyes, looking at the stern. Lymon and Sid were talking to each other. What was Sid Harness, the FBI agent, doing here? Was the Bureau involved now? A thousand questions were boiling inside her.

She caught the furtive glances they shot her way and literally itched to stomp back there and demand to know how they had found her, what they were doing in New York, and more to the point, why the hell they hadn't blown her cover.

"Jennifer?" Mary Abernathy asked, coming to sit on the bench next to her. "Are you all right?" She glanced back at the men, irritation in her eyes.

"Furious. Confused," Sheela admitted, falling back into her role. "They treat me like a baby."

"I've called ahead to make quarters available for them the way you requested." She paused. "We've put them in a suite next door to yours, but it's a waste of money. I promise you, you won't need your security. You'll be under the literal nose of our excellent protective services. You are more than welcome to order your people to return to shore. You'll have plenty of time to have them meet you at the dock when you return."

Sheela made a face as if mulling it over. "No, it's all right. They're just doing what I pay them for. It's just that sometimes..." She glanced up, eyes hollow and vulnerable. "You know, being rich isn't all that most people think. For me, it's like living in a cage. I can't just be normal. Everyone wants something from me."

After a pause, Mary asked, "I do have to know one thing: Are they discreet?"

Sheela answered with blunt honesty. "Believe me, there are times when I wish Lymon wasn't such a perfect damned professional."

"Well, don't worry about them." Mary watched the bridge pass overhead. "We have relations with a lot of clients who have privacy concerns. Believe me, many of them come with security details a great deal bigger and more cumbersome than yours."

"Thanks." She lowered her head, looking meek. "I'd better go back and make peace. I acted like a real shit. I tricked them in order to slip away."

"Then," Mary Abernathy mused, "how did they find you?"

"Something incredible, no doubt. Lymon's a magician. He probably pulled a white rabbit out of his hat and it ratted me out."

She got to her feet and took a moment to adjust to the pitch and roll of the launch as it rose and fell on the swells. The breeze was cool off the water, wind tugging at her brown wig. Seagulls hovered off the lee, watching to see if the incomprehensible humans had food.

To steady herself, Sheela kept one hand on the gunwale as she made her way astern. Sid cued Lymon, who turned, nodding, his face inscrutable.

"Lymon," she said wearily, "how the hell did you find me?"

He glanced toward where Mary Abernathy watched before returning his stare to the billowing white wake behind them. "Could you turn your back to those people while you're talking to me?"

"What?" She placed her hands on the fantail, complying. "Why?"

"Hell, Sheela, I don't know. Just a hunch. Who is that woman, the one with the beady little Attila eyes?"

"Mary Abernathy. She's a nurse. She came and checked me out, set up the appointment."

He shot her a worried look. "Just what the hell do you think you're doing?"

"First you tell me how you found me."

"You scared the shit out of Tomaso when you made him drive you to the airport. I think it was the disguise that weirded him out. He called and said you were up to something dangerous, that Felix was involved."

"Felix?" She lifted a hand to her throat.

"Yeah. By the way, despite his tough-guy image, it turns out that he's a real wimp when it comes to pain. And last but not least, you should clear the redial on your phone."

She considered what he'd said—not just the words, but the tone in his voice. She hated the flat control as if he were keeping a careful rein. When she looked hard into his eyes, she could see it brewing there: fear mixing with growing desperation.

Her chest tightened when he said, "Now it's my turn. What are you doing here? Why are you playing Jennifer Weaver games with Genesis Athena? What if they see through your brown hair and eyes? Why are you taking silly chances and putting yourself at risk?"

"I'm going right to their heart." She swallowed hard. "And when I get there, I'm going to rip it out."

"Holy shit," Sid whispered from Lymon's other side.

"Can you get out of it?" Lymon asked tersely. "Stop this nonsense before you get hurt?"

"Of course. I'm going to back out at the last minute. I'm going to say I just can't do it. That I'm not ready. I'll apologize in a most pathetic manner and maybe cry a little. I'll offer them a big enough settlement to make it all right, and then when I get back to LA, Felix is going to file suit. We're going to blow this thing wide open. And Christal's going to be part of the settlement."

"Assuming they don't find out about it," Sid muttered. "If Nancy Hartlee is any indication, these guys play for keeps."

Lymon shot his friend a nervous glance. "Yeah, I think you're right."

"What are you two talking about?" Sheela endured the threads of fear winding through her. "Damn it, Sid, are you here investigating for the FBI?"

"Well...yes and no." He made a wry face. "Actually, more no than yes. I'm just as far out on the wobbly limb as you are, Ms. Marks."

Lymon asked, "Where's this boat taking us?"

"To a ship," she told them, gesturing forward. "Somewhere out there in the ocean."

"And what happens once we get there?"

"Jennifer Weaver will supposedly have Genesis Athena impregnate her with a Sheela Marks's baby. I mean, I'm obviously not going through with the procedure, but don't you see? It's the proof we need to sue the shit out of these bastards. And that's where they do it. Out at sea on a ship."

"Damn it, Sheela! What if they figure out who you are? I know Felix did the background work and set this up, but so many things could go wrong. We're talking about real bad shit here."

"They'll never know, Lymon." What was supposed to be a reassuring smile died on her lips. "I know this role. I can do it in my sleep. I mean, who's to tell them? You and Sid surely won't say anything. Just play the part. Be yourselves. Big, tough, security guys."

"You're sure they'll let you walk out?" Sid asked

skeptically. He looked like a man with a bad feeling stuck sideways in his gut.

"Why wouldn't they?" Sheela shrugged. "To them, I'm a psychologically disturbed rich girl living on a bloated trust fund. At the last minute, I break down, change my mind, and say I won't do it. Trust me, it's in Jennifer's character. As long as they get paid, why would they care?"

"If they don't...if it goes bad," Lymon warned softly, "you be sure we're close. You understand?"

Sheela nodded, the thudding of fear beating at the base of her throat. That look of desperation in his eyes kept eroding more and more of her courage. "It'll be fine, Lymon. Trust me."

"A ship," Sid muttered. "An oceangoing laboratory where they do genetic procedures." He paused suddenly, stiffening. "You know, Nancy Hartlee was found floating right out here."

"You mentioned her before. Who's Nancy Hartlee?" Sheela put a hand to her roiling gut.

"One of Sid's missing geneticists." Lymon's worried eyes sent a tremor through her. "No one could figure out how she'd drowned so far offshore."

"It's all starting to make sense." Sid balled a fist, back hunched as if the muscles were taut. "Fuck!"

"Double fuck," Sheela said glumly.

"Yeah," Lymon agreed. "Times three."

CHAPTER 13

Hank had just finished a workout on the weight machine in the E Deck fitness center. He stepped out of the locker room showers. Reaching for one of the towels that rested on the rack, he buried his face in the soft terry. It was when he started on his head that he realized he wasn't alone. April stood brazenly, arms crossed, head cocked, right in the middle of the men's locker room.

She laughed, reading his sudden discomfort. "Why, I'm surprised at you." She stepped forward, using her fingertip to wipe up a droplet of water from his left nipple. He followed it as she raised it to her mouth and touched it to the tip of her tongue.

"Hey, sweetheart, it's not me. What if some other guy was in here? You might make him blush."

When her eyes met his it was with a feral curiosity. "And you don't blush?"

He pulled her to him, heedless of her expensive pantsuit, and kissed her hard. He could feel the strength in her body as she stiffened and arched against him. In the end, he let her push back. She gave him that fiery look, and his soul began to swell. Damn, she was saucy when she was mad.

She broke away, looking down. Her natty pantsuit was dampened over the breasts, belly, and thighs. "You bastard!"

Hank chuckled and continued toweling himself. He made sure she was watching as he spread his thighs and rolled the towel around his heat-distended genitals. "Hey, April, you come walking into the men's locker room, you take dangerous chances. Shit happens. Especially when male hormones have been loosened up in the gym."

She flipped her metal-red hair back and studied him through narrowed eyes. "So, you had a good workout?"

He tossed the towel into the hamper and turned to where his clothes were laid out across a bench. "I worry myself."

"No wonder." She was staring down at the wet spots. "Keep pulling shit like this...I'll kill you."

"April, I haven't felt this good in years." He stepped into his briefs and let the elastic snap around his waist. "I feel alive in a way that I never have. I'm doing something for the first time in my life."

"And what is that?" She reached for another of the towels, patting it on her breasts and belly to dry the stain.

"I'm working for me." He ran his arms into his shirt. "Better, I'm working for a team I can believe in. I mean, this isn't the Bureau. This is real. Results count, not political bullshit. I'm rested, I haven't spent the night worrying about a house payment, or what I'd done to piss fucking Marsha off, or whether I was in or out at the office."

April balled her towel and flung it at the hamper. "Pull your pants on. I want you to see something."

He zipped his jeans and tugged on his running shoes. When he stood, she was giving him that probing look. What was this shit? Was she about to pass judgment on him again? Part of his euphoria evaporated.

"I hate it when you start staring at me like that."

"I want your opinion on something."

"Why do I get the feeling I'm being set up?"

She grinned at him, stepping close and lancing a long fingernail under his chin; a predatory curiosity lay behind the expanded pupils in her gray eyes. "I can't say for certain, but my guess is that you'll like it."

He trapped her finger, pulled it up to his lips, and kissed the tip as he traded gaze for gaze. "Lead forth."

He followed as April led the way to the door and pushed it open. She took his arm, pulling it around her shoulder. "I've booked the movie room for us. First off, there's something I want you to see. Second, it'll give my clothes time to dry, and third, it will give me time to decide if I still want to slap the shit out of you."

He grinned where she couldn't see it.

"Sexy movie? You know, males are visually stimulated."

"No shit? Bam! Revelation! After all these years, I finally understand why men go completely brainless when they see my tits. Until now, I thought it was just some bizarre form of innate stupidity."

She stopped at the movie room door and let him push it open. Hank stepped inside, surprised to find Neal Gray in one of the seats.

"Hey, Hank."

"What's up, Neal?"

"More of the same. We're still trying to gauge damage control on the Anaya thing." He glanced at April, eyes fixing on her damp breasts. "What happened to you?"

"Don't ask."

"It would never cross my mind." He waved at the screen. "We'll fast-forward through the meaningless parts. Have a seat, guys."

Hank settled himself into one of the comfortable chairs. April couldn't be too pissed at him, because she slid in beside him. The lights dimmed, and the big screen that filled one wall illuminated as cameras followed April and a woman that Hank immediately recognized as Christal into what appeared to be a small but elegant locker room.

"This was taken this morning," Neal said. "It's part of a film the marketing team will be using for our 'Zea' series."

"Huh?" Hank asked, watching as April's screen voice said, *"If you'll remove your clothes and open that locker on the right, you'll see that we've taken the liberty of supplying you with a wardrobe. I think the size is right."*

Neal replied, "Zea is a series of females we'll be producing from Anaya's DNA. Now, obviously, we're not going to call them the 'Christal' series. If she chooses to settle, we'd rather not have her coming back asking for royalty in the future."

Hank watched the on-screen April say, *"I'm going for a swim."* Christal watched skeptically as April slipped off her shoes and began undressing. *"Like I said, we've got an hour. Use it any way you'd like. Me, I'm taking it in the pool."*

Hank glanced at April. "You told her no cameras."

"She'll never know. The Sheik arrived this morning. He wanted a chance to look over his investment. What you can't see is that the shower room has a one-way mirrored wall through which this was filmed. The same with the pool. Underwater cameras are hidden behind the lights. It's quite a sophisticated system. Top-of-the-line technology."

They watched Christal stare suspiciously around the room, sometimes peering straight into the camera. She checked the locker, hesitated, then reluctantly undressed. Hank swallowed hard, watching her as she padded to the door to stare longingly at the shower where April washed.

"We kept her in pretty Spartan quarters," April said. "She was ready for the opportunity."

The view changed as Christal stepped into the shower room, glancing in surprise at the camera. "She's just discovered the mirrored wall," April added with amusement. "Marketing is going to love that expression of wonder and awe. It gives her a sense of excitement, don't you think?"

Hank shifted as the camera closed on Christal's body. He might have screwed her, but he'd never seen her naked before. It was like Christmas—April and Christal, side by side for comparison: April, a little more full-breasted, pale with a dancer's supple body, beside long-limbed Christal, darker, brown, muscular, and lithe.

April and Neal laughed when April stepped out and Christal immediately scurried out to try the locker room door. "Now," Neal added, "tell me that wasn't expected?"

When Christal finally took the plunge, the camera angles changed again, following her as she crossed the poolside at a run and dove. Immediately, the underwater lenses picked her up, her perfect body lancing into the frame in a rush of white bubbles.

Hank fought the urge to shift again as the camera zoomed in on Christal's body, then backed away as April slipped past with eel-like grace. He could feel April's curious glance and tried to keep his expression nonchalant.

"This is what we want your opinion on," Neal said.

The cameras changed, focusing on Christal's face as April discussed the relative merits of Genesis Athena.

"Watch her," April added. "Study her closely, and tell me what you think."

Christal listened to April's comparison between the US government and Genesis Athena.

April leaned close to ask, "Is she buying it?"

"It's irritating her. You can see it in her mouth."

"Watch this." April indicated the screen as Christal declared: *"There's nothing I can do about what the government does with my tax dollars."*

"Bullshit," April shot back. *"You've just made that particular deal with the devil, Christal. You're comfortable with it."*

Hank leaned forward, watching Christal's familiar expression. The clarity of the picture was awesome. He could see her pupils, the faintest of tension at the corners of her mouth. He saw the reaction. "There! You got to her when you brought up the government funding of bad guys."

A moment later, he saw her expression turn thoughtful again when April told her that it would be cheaper to deep-six her, but that they wouldn't. "She's chewing on that."

He watched as Christal, oblivious now, climbed up out of the pool. Her face was pensive as she walked poolside to the showers. Damn, she was one fine-looking woman.

"Marketing is going to like this part," Neal added. "You can see her natural grace, here. She's vulnerable, but looking intelligent."

The scene shifted to the shower room. Hank watched as the women showered, the discussion continuing.

He started when April reached over on-screen and touched the wall. "What the...?"

Beside him, she laughed in amusement. "It's a big blow dryer. I'll take you sometime. You wouldn't believe how stimulating it is."

I believe!

He couldn't help gaping like an idiot as Christal's skin moved as if massaged. It did the most marvelous things with her breasts and belly. The air pressure gave her face an exotic look, sharpening her cheeks, black hair rippling out in a wave. Her narrowed eyes added to the effect, like something from an animator's pen. When it stopped, he was rigid in his seat, hands clasped on the armrests.

"This is the important part," Neal said. Was that a tremor in his voice? The man would have to be made of wood not to have been affected.

Hank managed to breathe again as he watched Christal and April dressing.

"Here!" Neal called as April asked what it would take.

Christal took a moment to consider. *"Five million."*

April's laugh was mocking. *"Not a chance."*

With an evaluative stare, Christal asked, *"So, what's your counteroffer?"*

"Two hundred thousand."

The camera was centered on Christal's expression when she said, *"What makes you think I wouldn't take it and spill my guts later anyway?"*

On-screen, April told her, *"Because we're a business, Anaya. You have a basic understanding of our capabilities, resources, and resolve. I think you know that we'll use them if we have to. We'll keep our end of the bargain only as long as you keep yours."*

After a thoughtful hesitation, Christal said, *"I'll think about it."*

The screen went blank and the lights came up. Neal turned in his chair. "You know her, Hank. Will she buy it, or do we go with the Jamaica option?"

Images of Christal's body undulating in the wind stream dominated his thoughts. *Shit!* "I don't know."

"Want to see it again?" April asked slyly, her gaze half-lidded and knowing.

See it again? Hell, he'd be dreaming that vision for the rest of his life!

"Actually, yeah. She'll go for it if it's handled right." Knowing full well she wouldn't.

He frowned. What in the hell had prompted him to say that?

"Paybacks are a bitch," Neal quipped. "And Gregor has made sure she'll never forget."

"Come on," April said, standing and reaching down

to pull Hank to his feet. “I need to go to my cabin. Some hairy ape spoiled my outfit.”

He stood, hoping his knees weren’t wobbly. April’s lips curled, reading his weakness. The excitement in her hooded gray eyes added to the stirring in his loins. It was shaping up to be an exciting afternoon.

CHAPTER 14

The *ZoeGen* looked huge as the launch motored into the ship's lee and the engines reversed. The only thing on the empty ocean, it might have been its own continent. Lymon glanced up, watching a platform and ladder lower from a hatch that opened in the great ship's side.

Dear God, I hope this was a good idea.

Setting foot aboard that ship went against every instinct. He reached down for the handles on his locked plastic case.

Sheela looked pale despite her makeup and brown wig. She gave him an uncertain smile, as if the reality of what she had plunged them into was dropping home like an anvil.

"This is going to be interesting," Sid muttered. He'd been on the verge of seasickness for most of the trip.

The launch rose and fell, rubbing on fenders as it came to rest beside the lowered landing. While the huge bulk of the ship blocked the prevailing wind and the swells, it still appeared dubious to Sid.

"If you'll each just wait until the surfaces match," one of the deckhands said, "we'll have you step right across."

Lymon met Sheela's wide-eyed stare with an encouraging smile. "Want to go back now?"

She shook her head too fast. "See it through."

"It's your call."

They watched as one by one the other passengers climbed up, held the handrails, and easily made the crossing. After the two pregnant women, Sheela took her turn, stepping across as the launch rose. One of the *ZoeGen's* crew women steadied her hand, then gestured her up the short set of steps to the hatch.

Lymon tightened his grip on the black plastic case, climbed up, and declined the young woman's hand as he made it. He turned back, calling, "It's easy."

"What if I miss?" Sid replied.

"The water's only a thousand feet deep here. You'll have lots of time to think about it on the way down. And once you're there, it'll be so dark you won't be able to see just how bad your situation really is."

"Asshole!"

Lymon climbed the steps, his case in hand, and glanced back just in time to see Sid scurry from the launch's deck to the platform.

The passageway that Lymon entered might have been a hallway at the Four Seasons. Sheela was waiting beside a uniformed crewman—a smiling young man this time. He wore a neat blue jacket with brass buttons, white pressed pants, and held his hands clasped before him. His name tag read PETER.

The young man was saying, "Everything is ready,

Ms. Weaver. As soon as you wish, we can proceed to your quarters and get you settled in."

"The luggage?" Lymon asked.

"That will be delivered by our staff. Would you like me to take that case for you, sir?"

"Thanks, but this is my responsibility." He gave Peter a *You know how it is* smile.

"Thank God! This thing doesn't move." Sid came barging in, muttering under his breath and looking green. Lymon noticed that perspiration was beading on his forehead.

"He's the last of our party," Sheela said in her irritated Jennifer tone. "We can go now."

Lymon took up station behind and to Sheela's right. Sid, not knowing the drill—or too close to puking—just followed along. Lymon could hear him sucking great gulps of air. Sometimes that even helped.

Despite the opulent nature of the corridor they followed, Lymon noted that small security cameras had been tastefully incorporated into the decor. Which got him to thinking: What if they had to get out of here in a hurry? A knot was pulling tight in his gut.

"You going to be any good if we land in the shit?" Lymon muttered over his shoulder.

"Point me in the right direction," Sid mumbled, "and I'll throw up all over them."

They entered a wood-paneled lift trimmed in polished brass. Sheela was fidgeting around in her purse, muttering, "My compact. God, I didn't forget my compact!"

"We have a well-stocked commissary," the steward told her. "And the launch makes several round trips each day. Feel free to contact me if you need anything at all." He gave them a professional smile. "Some of our clients have been known to charter a helicopter just to go to dinner ashore."

Lymon kept his face straight as Sheela stopped her rooting and glanced up. "What? You don't have food?"

"Oh, we have a gourmet chef and a full kitchen. Your people even approved a menu for your stay. Once you're settled, we can go over it. If there are any changes you would like to make, we'll be happy to accommodate them."

The lift opened and Lymon stepped out, checking the corridor. He made way for Sheela, glaring at Sid, who was still sentient enough to realize Lymon was trying to tell him something. With a hand signal Lymon put him into position as they started down an even fancier hallway, the wood here looking like teak. The polish was so deep he could see his reflection.

"This will be your quarters for the next week," the steward said as he stopped before a door on the left and opened it. Lymon followed Sheela inside and promptly stepped around her, surveying the room. This was the only advance he was going to get.

The place was large, airy, perhaps twenty by thirty feet with a ten-foot ceiling paneled in skylights framed by thick black timbers. The furniture looked Victorian, with polished wood and expensive fabric. Concessions to the twenty-first century included a big-screen home theater unit as sophisticated as Sheela's own that dominated one wall. A computer desk stood in one comer with a monitor, keyboard, and fax/printer looking like they'd just been lifted out of a corporate office. A cordless phone sat in its cradle. Where the floor was exposed beyond the thick red carpet, it was waxed wood. Two large picture windows filled the opposite wall, and a weather door let out onto a spacious balcony. Lymon checked the door, leaving it for later. He walked across the suite, noting the ornate wet bar in the corner, and opened the corner door that accessed the bedroom. Behind him the steward began explaining the bar's capabilities and demonstrating the refrigerator and microwave to Sheela.

Lymon found a king-size bed atop a boxed frame. Another phone rested on the nightstand along with a TV remote for the OLED screen on the far wall. An alcove to the right was fitted out with a settee that allowed its occupant to stare out over the ocean through a huge glass window. In the bedroom, Lymon quickly went through the built-in dresser drawers, checked the nightstands, and stepped into the spacious bathroom. He found white marble tiling and counters, golden faucets, a whirlpool tub, and a glassed-in shower. A gleaming toilet stood next to the bidet. The towels were clean and perfectly folded, and the toilet paper was full in the gold-plated holder.

A quick look over the place showed nothing amiss. But, as Anaya would have said, his whiskers were vibrating. It looked like any of the luxury suites Sheela had occupied around the world. Why then, did he have this uneasy feeling of hidden threat?

He walked back through to the main room and found the steward involved in teaching Sheela the intricacies of the TV remote.

Sid was out on the balcony. Lymon stepped out, looking around. "Feeling better?"

"Yeah." Sid had leaned on the rounded steel of the

railing. "Funny, looking at the ocean doesn't bother me from up here."

"Glad you're recovering. You're not acting up to snuff for the security business." He looked around, taking in the deck chairs and tables. Over the side, he found a straight drop down to the ocean, what, eighty feet below? Leaning out, he could see that another balcony was below, while a deck railing appeared to be just above.

"Nice digs." Sid stuffed his hands in his pockets and looked around.

"Come on. You're going to learn the security business."

Lymon led the way back in and managed to catch the steward's attention. "Excuse me, Peter, could we have a quick word with you?"

"Sure." The steward stepped over while Sheela was stabbing at the remote.

Lymon gave the man his best smile. "Could you contact your head of security and set up an appointment as soon as possible? We'd also like a map of the ship, something detailing the various decks and corridors with escape routes, directions to the dining room, and other venues highlighted. We need to know the location of the closest lifeboats, personal flotation devices, medical facilities, fire extinguishers, and first aid kits. I'd also like a list of shipboard contacts for emergencies, phone numbers for medical personnel, security, your equivalent of a concierge, and room service. We would like a schedule of Ms. Weaver's planned activities and a schematic of where they are to take place. If you could provide us with a list of other guests aboard, and their security personnel, I would be happy to meet—"

"Whoa!" The steward threw his hands up. "I'll have Neal Gray, our head of security, contact you as soon as he can."

"Thanks." Lymon backed off, slipping the steward a fifty-dollar bill.

Sid had taken that in, wide-eyed. He followed Lymon over to the wet bar in the corner. As Lymon began sorting through the stock of drinks, snacks, and accessories, Sid whispered, "A fifty? Are you nuts?"

Lymon gave him a subtle grin as he continued his inspection, making sure the packaging hadn't been tampered with and that the bottles still had their factory seals. "If I have to ask this guy for a box of Cracker Jack, he's going to move mountains to find it for me."

"He'd have probably done it for ten."

"Maybe." Lymon shrugged. "If we were lodging on D Deck downstairs. But up here on B Deck, we might just end up needing more than Cracker Jack before we're out of here. You get my drift?"

"Uh, maybe."

"What if Shee...Ms. Weaver decides at three in the morning that she wants to blow this berg? How much cooperation am I going to get from Pete?"

"I'm starting to catch on. So, what's next?"

"I want you to go over this room carefully. See what's here. Memorize this suite and then we'll take a walk and learn our way around. You need to be familiar enough with the ship that you can find your way around in an emergency without floundering."

Pete had taken Sheela on a tour of the bedroom.

“Our job,” Lymon continued, “is to be ready for any contingency. Normally we figure this out in advance, meeting the people, touring the facilities, and learning the picky little details. The rule here is that we hurry a little harder since we’re behind.” He dropped his voice. “And you defer to any of *Ms. Weaver’s* demands.”

“Right,” Sid said, catching on. He still didn’t look fit, but at least his mind was working again. “What’s your initial take, boss?”

“Something’s not right about this place.”

“Yeah, I’m starting to think that, too.”

“Think of it as a crime scene, Sid. Look this place over with the same care you would use at the scene of a triple homicide.”

“Got it. I just hope you’re not being prophetic.”

CHAPTER 15

Using Nancy Hartlee's nanotechnology always delighted Gregor McEwan. He'd tried to score with the lady in the first couple of months after she'd been brought to Yemen. Back in those days, before the *ZoeGen,* they'd been a small, tightly bound nucleus of brainpower stuck on the edge of the Arabian desert. A camaraderie had built among them, and despite the reality of their incarceration, it had been a period of incredible cross-fertilization of ideas, theories, and conceptual applications.

He and Nancy had hit it off, at least until she began to grasp just how brilliant he really was. Perhaps if she'd stuck with him instead of walking out, she'd be sharing in the glory. Instead, Nancy Hartlee was dead and buried, while no less than fifteen of her little clones were spread here and there around the world. Several had been placed in scientific-oriented families to see if her doppelgängers developed the same keen brain. That was one of the fascinating things: seeing how the duplicates developed. Talk about a laboratory for behavioral genetics.

Gregor concentrated on the image projected on the screen. His fingers turned the knobs that manipulated the nanoscalpel, the cellular dam, and pipette. In the pale green image, the cell appeared something like a translucent jellyfish. The oocyte's organelles were defined by diffracted infrared light to minimize cellular photosensitivity. The photons in turn were intensified and converted into the screen image.

The nanoscalpel methodically slit the structures of the cellular wall before Gregor turned the knob that directed the nanodam into place. Another of Nancy's inventions, it kept the cytoplasm from sagging and losing its integrity. To date, he was the only person who insisted on calling it a speculum. Well, it was an egg, wasn't it?

Using the nanodam he eased the cytoplasm aside and made another incision through the layers of the endoplasmic reticulum. In many ways, this was the trickiest part. The ER, as they called it, had the same qualities as corrugated paper, and was just about as delicate. If too much pressure was applied, it could fold up on itself, destroying its integrity and damaging the cell's ability to function. The ER had to be eased open to expose the nuclear membrane before inserting the nanodam. Doing so was more of an art than a science, and over the years, Gregor had developed a feel for the equipment that remained unmatched, although Ibrahim was getting close.

Finally, he had the nucleus exposed. Using a grease pencil on the screen, he marked the orientation of the nucleolus in relation to the centrioles, the poles to which the chromosomes attached for meiotic division. Only then did he insert the micropipette to the nuclear wall. Applying light suction, he turned the nucleus, watching it move in relation to the centrioles. Reaching out on the control board, Gregor changed the image perspective to the rear. With a dial he inserted a nanopipette to the backside of the nuclear membrane. Then, as he began retraction of the nucleus through the incision, he slowly pumped purified, anaerobic, neutral pH water into the space created by the retreating nucleus.

Having successfully extracted the nucleus, he retracted it and spun the controls that brought the replacement into position. This he eased forward into the incision and, encountering the water-filled nuclear cavity, reversed suction, allowing vacuum to pull the new nucleus into the cavity. All that remained was to spin the nucleus so that its orientation with the centrioles was as close to the original's as the new nuclear morphology would allow.

Gregor smiled with a delighted sense of satisfaction when he withdrew the pipettes and nanodam. Changing the angle on the screen, he compared the images. The organelles near the incision had a three percent variation from their original location.

Gregor rolled his chair back from the control panel and jotted his observations and procedures into the master notebook. Under the bottom, he wrote the word SUCCESSFUL! and underlined it twice. All the oocyte needed now was a dash of PLCs and a nutrient-rich uterine wall to stick to.

"Sir?" Ibrahim said, leaning into the room. "Something has come up that we think you should see."

"Indeed?"

"Yes, sir." Ibrahim was in his late twenties, darker than the rest of the Sheik's kin, with a profound brain. He was the most adept of the trainees and Gregor's personal favorite. "It is either a most remarkable coincidence, or someone has done something very wrong."

CHAPTER 16

BBC World News was playing on the lounge television. Christal sat on one of the couches, her right leg pulled up, a magazine in her hands. Had she been asked, she couldn't have said what had been on the news, nor could she have even named the magazine in her slim brown fingers. Instead, she stared absently across the empty room, running the events of the morning through her mind.

Movement at the corner of her eye caused her to stir. Brian Everly had leaned his head in. "There you are! Missed you in the cafeteria. Hungry?"

She smiled, and felt it slip away. "No. But I probably ought to eat."

He had stepped into the room. "What? New clothes? Don't tell me you made a trip to the QVC in Sydney for a little shopping while I wasn't looking?"

She closed the magazine and tossed it onto the coffee table in front of her. "No. I had a little adventure this morning. Copperhead came to take me upstairs—allegedly for a meeting, but I'm not so sure anymore."

"Copperhead?"

"April Hayes."

"Ah?" He stepped around the coffee table and seated himself at the far end of the couch. "How much did they offer, and for what?"

"Two hundred thousand to drop any charges and keep my mouth shut."

He wove his fingers together. "You going to take it?"

"How the hell do I know?"

The worry that had been churning in her gut rose to the surface. "What are my options, Brian? If I say no, do you think they're going to let me spend the rest of my life down here eating their food, taking up space, and being a security risk?"

"Then take it and be glad." He stared down at his hands. "But if you do, Christal, don't ever, ever say a word. Not to anyone. Not ever."

She gave him a sidelong glance. "You think they'd really do it? Pay me and let me go?"

He gave her a weary smile. "For whatever reason, they'd rather have you outside and mum, rather than dead."

"Copperhead said that they'd rather pay now than later. I can understand that. People will begin asking questions when I don't reappear. I left them some information, you see. And I'd had run-ins with Copperhead that involved the police. That's a lot of loose ends."

"Take it, Christal."

She turned suspicious eyes on him. "Why, Brian? You part of this?"

The weary smile deepened. "I'd expect smarter

questions from a woman as bright as you, Christal Anaya, but no, not in the way you think."

"How, then?" Why hadn't she noticed what a handsome man he was? She liked the gentle concern in his odd pale eyes, the easy way that he sat. Something about him made her feel comfortable when she was in his presence.

"Because I'd rather have you safe."

It was the tone in his voice, the way he managed to shyly avoid her eyes.

"Gallantry?"

The faintest of shrugs lifted his shoulders. Then he laughed at himself and sat forward to rub his hands together. They were muscular hands, eminently male, veined, with strong tendons.

"I might even go with you."

"What?" She tried to see past the careful expression on his face.

"I've never had a reason to join them."

"What are you talking about?"

"I've been here for five years." He turned sad eyes on her. "They took me out of my car and stole me away from my life. They locked me up here and put me to work, making sure I knew that I either produced, or they would destroy me. I watched colleagues wither and die in this place. Here, and at the lab in Yemen, we rewrote the rules. We changed the bloody world as it hasn't been changed since the first atomic bomb detonated in your New Mexico."

He gestured toward the BBC anchorwoman who talked so thoughtfully into the camera. "They don't understand. Nothing's the same. Within thirty years, people will be ordering their children like they do motor cars."

"Come on."

Ironic humor tugged at his lips. "Color is one of the easier options: white, brown, or black? We also mix and match for any shade in-between. We have a special on eyes this month. Personally, I like yours. Oh, right! Then we have strength. Do you want fast or slow muscle?"

"Huh?"

"By programming for a preponderance of slow myosin— that's one of the contractive muscle proteins —we can make your child a world-class weightlifter. If you want a sprinter, we can change the DNA to produce fast Two-a and Two-x myosins. You, incidentally, have a preponderance of slow myosin. You're better at endurance over the long run. I'd like the chance to test that out one of these days."

"That's a joke, right? About the muscles, I mean."

"Sorry. Fact is, it's one of the simple qualities we can tailor into your child. Other things, like resistance to a communicable disease, get a bit more dicey. Something that people don't understand is that in nature, everything becomes a trade-off. If we tinker with the immunogenetics to build a resistance to certain gram-negative streptococcal bacteria on one hand, we increase susceptibility to infectious bacilli on the other. What is taken in one place, must be given back somewhere else."

"Good God, you're not joking."

"You, my dear Christal, have a susceptibility to multiple sclerosis. I'm not saying that you're going to get it—odds are that you won't—but with the right preconditions, the proper viral vector, and a stressed immune system, you could. It's because of a protein inconsistency in the myelin sheath in your nerves. It's easily fixable so that your descendants won't have it."

She shifted, tensing. "You found that in that sample of mine you've been working on?"

He glanced away again. "We fixed your disposition to osteoarthritis, too. It was a simple base-pair substitution that will add elasticity to the hyaline cartilage. On the other hand, I did nothing to change your sebaceous and maxillary glands."

"Huh?"

"I like the way you smell, Anaya."

"Madre de Dios!"

"Sorry, I guess I shouldn't have said that."

She reached out, laying a slim hand on his arm. "I'm a little stunned is all. Talk about Alice through the looking glass. One minute I'm running an investigation in LA and the next I'm talking to the Cheshire Cat."

She shook her head. "I don't understand. These things you're doing? Stealing DNA, changing it? Curing diseases and selling babies? How come no one is screaming their head off? Where's the church? What's the Pope say? Where's the righteous indignation of the president, the senators, and Congress? *Why doesn't anybody care?"*

"Easy, Anaya." He reached out and caught the balled fist she was clenching.

She stared angrily into his eyes. "Well?"

He gave a paternal smile that soothed some of the ruffle in her feathers. "You know Senator Baber? The one on the Senate ethics committee?"

"Tennessee, right?"

"I think so. He was here last year."

"Huh?"

"We cloned a new prostate for him. His old one was enlarged and precancerous. The story I heard was that he'd rather have a new one than lose his sexual potency."

"Cloned a new prostate? Wait a minute! Nobody transplants prostates."

"He had to fly to our facility in Yemen for the procedure."

"Sexual potency? He's sixty!"

"The young lady accompanying him—I think he called her a 'staffer'—wasn't nearly that old." His smile widened. "If you'll recall, Baber's wife died of amyotrophic lateral sclerosis. You would know that better as Lou Gehrig's disease. It's not a pretty way to go, and it tore Baber apart. So, at the same time we implanted his new prostate, we did a simple gene scan on his daughter, Marissa. On her twenty-first chromosome, we found a missense mutation at the q22.1 location—a SOD1 condition for the autosomal dominant trait."

"That's not English," Christal objected.

"Oh, yes, right. Sorry. It means she got the ALS gene from her mother and it would override its allele. That's the functioning gene from her father's chromosome. In short, she was perhaps five years from the onset of the disease, so we ran a gene therapy, using CRISPER and a tailored viral vector to replace the malfunctioning gene. As time passes, the inserted gene will produce enough enzymes to break down the toxins that cause ALS. Baber won't have to watch his daughter die in agony the way his wife did."

"So, what are you saying?"

"I'm saying that just like my example with bacterial resistance earlier demonstrated, what you lose on one hand, is taken on the other. In short, do you expect world leaders to decry Genesis Athena in public while in private we're restoring the gift of life to them and their loved ones?"

Christal sat back. "But these other things."

"What?" Brian lifted his hand as a supplicant. "You're drooling mad that they're going to sell your DNA? That people like me have been held against our wills? Do you think that Senator Baber is going to call out the dogs? Genesis Athena gave him back his sex and his daughter. Where do you think he's going to come down?"

"There are other leaders."

"Ah? The director of your FBI had a procedure done at Bethesda Naval Hospital last year, remember?"

"Yes. Something about deterioration of the optic nerve. After a couple of months, he was back to twenty-twenty vision."

"Want to take a stab at who licensed that procedure? That was actually our beloved Gregor's brainchild. He was the one who thought to utilize that particular protein matrix for delivery to the degenerating cells. The point being that if push came to shove, would your FBI director have his heart and balls behind an investigation of Genesis Athena?" He paused. "Gregor even hinted that your director may have been responsible for your friend Hank's recruitment. Well, for the initial phone call at least."

At her stunned look, he added, "It's more than just the *ZoeGen,* Christal. It's hospitals, pharmaceuticals, gene therapies, and a thousand patents in molecular biology. The tentacles extend throughout the medical field. They offer life and hope where there hasn't been before."

"So, what do we do?"

He stared down at his hands again. "I've spent five years fighting them, and what's it got me? My friends are gone, my life has been stolen, and my universe is this little patch of deck in the guts of the *ZoeGen.*" He reached out, tentatively touching her hair. "For the first time, I've found something that I want. A reason to finally say all right, take their bloody settlement, and go someplace to try to rebuild my life."

She didn't understand at first. The sadness mixed with hope deep in his eyes sent a flutter through her. "God, Brian, you hardly know me."

"Right. And I'm not trying to be a boor. A woman like you has guys hitting on her all the time. It's not like that. From the moment I first saw you, all hot and sweaty, I was stopped short in my tracks." He withdrew his hand. "But, no matter what, take their offer, Christal. For me. Get the hell out of here, bite your bloody tongue, and be glad of having your life back."

"What about you?"

He looked away. "Assuming they actually believe me, I'd like to look you up out there. On the outside. When there's just the two of us. You know, maybe do dinner and the movies. Just to see if I find you so wondrously attractive as I do in this bloody hole." A shrug. "I want a chance to be normal with you, that's all."

"You don't think they'll let you go?"

"I fought them a long time, Christal. McEwan once

told me he'd see me rot in hell before I'd breathe unfiltered air."

She bit her lip, frowning as she considered. "No matter what, Brian, I'm not leaving here without you."

"Now that," McEwan's familiar voice interrupted, "might be quite a feat."

They turned to see McEwan leaning in the door. He stepped in, one eyebrow raised. "Thinking about leaving? Really?"

Brian sighed wearily. "Oddly, I've been trying to talk Ms. Anaya into accepting the offer she's been made." His voice dropped. "I've been thinking of accepting, too."

"You, Brian?" McEwan's voice mocked. "After all your years of protestation and principle?"

Brian's soft chuckle was heavy with resignation. "What am I going to do? Sit here in the bowels of this ship for the rest of my life? You've won, McEwan. You and Genesis Athena." He paused as McEwan studied his expression. "I'm tired."

"Yes," McEwan agreed. "I suppose you are. But why should we believe that you'll play by our rules?"

"Maybe because I've never had a reason before."

McEwan turned his attention to Christal, as if seeing her anew. She tensed under his probing eyes. He said, "Ibrahim and I were just running a few tests on a blood and tissue sample taken from a client. You know, to test for compatibility? We've just made a fascinating discovery. Too bad you weren't there, Brian."

"Oh?"

McEwan's eyes hadn't left Christal's face. "The client is already aboard. A Ms. Jennifer Weaver here for an implantation. That name mean anything to you?"

Christal caught herself, struggling to keep her face straight. *Jennifer Weaver?*

"No." Brian answered absently, "Should it?"

"Maybe not now, but she's going to make history soon. She's here for a Sheela Marks copy."

Christal imagined Sheela's face staring down from the screen. *For a Sheela Marks implant?* Sheela hadn't come here, had she? Dear God, was she aboard the *ZoeGen*?

"Oh, it's a little coincidental, that's all." McEwan's eyes never wavered. "We've just never seen a perfect match between a client and a donor before. It was one hundred percent the same. Right down to point mutations."

Brian sounded perplexed. "That's impossible!"

"Yes. Quite."

Christal's heart began to hammer. She had no idea what McEwan was reading from her expression. Jennifer Weaver? God, it had to be! Was Lymon with her? Had they tracked her down? If so, then it was only a matter of time until the cavalry appeared.

"There's got to be a mistake," Brian said irritably. "Someone mixed the samples. It's a joke."

"Oh, it's not a joke." McEwan smiled at Christal with a subtle satisfaction. "As Ms. Anaya will be able to tell you soon enough, I have a very sophisticated sense of humor. One with a wee bit o' time delay."

Brian was frowning as McEwan turned on his heel and strode from the room.

"What was that all about?" Christal tried to control her racing pulse.

"The bit about time delay? I have no idea, but

there's only one way a donor and client can have a perfect match."

She placed a hand on his arm, chafing under the scrutiny of the security cameras. Would they be watching her? Recording her reaction? "Explain."

"Prior to beginning the process of implanting an embryo into a host mother, we do a series of simple tests to determine compatibility. The first thing we look at is blood type, since blood is the interface between mother's uterus and the fetal placenta. We want to know if Rh is a factor, as well as any of a number of other genetic predispositions in the immune system. If we find no conflicts, our physicians will give the woman a complete physical, and inject her to stimulate ovulation and the release of multiple oocytes, egg cells from the ovaries. After we collect the eggs, we'll evaluate them for morphology and resources, choose the best, and replace the nuclear DNA with the donor's."

"Yes, I know all that. What did McEwan mean they matched?"

"Christal, the only way they can match one hundred percent is if they come from the same person."

She felt the blood draining from her face. "Brian, we've got to talk." She glanced meaningfully up at the camera. "There's got to be a place."

CHAPTER 17

When Peter finished with Sheela, he looked at Lymon and Sid, asking, "Would you gentlemen like to see your room?"

Lymon, Sid in tow, followed Peter down the B Deck hall to the next suite. This proved to be a duplicate of Sheela's, right down to the stock of fine liquors in the bar.

"Is this right?" Lymon asked. "Generally quarters for security are somewhat, well, less expensive."

Pete clasped his hands, his perfect professional smile unblemished. "This was done at Ms. Weaver's request, sir. If you would like other quarters, we would be more than happy to comply, but as I'm sure you can understand, it will have to come through her."

"I'm sure this will be fine, Peter." He slipped another fifty from his money clip and handed it over. "Thank you very much for your courtesy to Ms. Weaver."

"Thank you, sir. Is there anything else?"

"No, that will be all."

Sid, in the meantime, had taken to wandering around the room, looking carefully at the walls and ornamentation. "Quite the digs. I could get used to this business." A hesitation. "Uh, that is if you think I work out, sir."

At the old familiar tone in his voice, Lymon turned wary. "It's not always like this."

"I would hope not," Sid added cryptically as he turned away from one of the wall sconces. "Uh, you said something about checking out the corridors? Getting the lay of the land? Maybe we'd better be doing that."

"I did." Lymon bent, laying his plastic case on the table. As he began undoing the combination lock, Sid leaned close to whisper, "If there's anything there you don't want seen, you'd better not open it."

Lymon froze, reading Sid's eyes. "Right." Instead, he strode over to the phone and lifted the receiver.

"Operator. How may I help you?"

"Ms. Weaver's suite, please."

On the second ring, Sheela answered, *"Hello?"*

"Ms. Weaver, it's Lymon. We'll be advancing the hallways. If you need anything, please ring my pager."

"Thank you, Lymon. Sometime soon I must talk to you. We have some things to clear up."

"Yes, ma'am." He tried to sound contrite and hung up. Looking at Sid, he said, "Let's go."

He was turning when a knock sounded. Lymon met Sid's curious gaze and shrugged. Opening the door, he admitted an attractive man in a gray suit, white shirt, and tie. The blond hair had been combed back to reveal a high forehead. He had a professional smile under his wary blue eyes.

"Hello. I'm Neal Gray, head of *ZoeGen* security."

Lymon hesitated for the slightest instant and recovered immediately as he recognized the guy. He'd last seen him in the parking lot outside Christal's Marriott. Lymon forced his most bluff smile, extending his hand. "Lymon Bridges, and my partner, Sid Harness. We work for June Rosen's security firm. Glad to meet you."

The man's shake was firm as Lymon searched his eyes for any hint of recognition. Would he know him? Lymon had been wearing a three-quarter helmet that night, with a full-face visor. While Gray's face had been clearly visible in the sodium lights, how much of his own could have been seen?

"What can we do for you, Mr. Bridges? I came just as soon as I could after receiving Peter's call. I trust everything's been satisfactory so far."

"It has. You have excellent staff." Lymon thrust his hands into his pockets. "We just wanted to introduce ourselves. Familiarize ourselves with your system and see if there was anything we could do to make your job easier."

"We appreciate that. Peter should have shown you your rooms. If you have a minute, why don't we take a tour of the ship? Your advance, if you will."

"We'd like that." Lymon kept his smile in place. "After you."

They followed Gray out into the hallway as the man said, "In all honesty, I don't think you guys are going to have much to do. Believe me, we've got all the bases covered. Consider this assignment as having your own semi-private cruise ship. And since your principal was gracious enough to provide a suite, I think you're going to enjoy your stay."

"Are we expected to share the king bed?" Sid asked dourly, eyes hooded.

"Peter didn't tell you? The love seat across from the TV folds out. Or we could have a second bed brought up."

"The foldout will be fine." Sid grinned humorlessly. "Boss, I'd actually prefer the foldout."

"That's it, suck up," Lymon chided, trying to stay in character.

Gray pointed at the hallway. "I'm sure you've already noticed that we have security cameras up and down the hallways. As a result we can control movement and access through any part of the visitors' portion of the ship. B Deck is yours to roam, gentlemen. Please feel free to use any of the facilities. We have a weight and exercise room." He pointed to a door marked with a golden barbell. "The nearest fire extinguishers are at either end of the hallway."

"What about first aid?" Lymon asked.

"You didn't bring a kit?" Gray asked innocently.

"In my suitcase," Lymon replied dryly.

"As I thought." Gray clasped his hands together. "Dial zero on any phone. The operator is on duty twenty-four/seven. Simply state the nature of the medical emergency and your location. Two trained EMTs will be on site within minutes if not seconds. Because of the nature of our work, we have a small hospital on board. We can handle anything from heart attacks to hangnails."

"Quite an operation."

"You'd be surprised." The man's voice was filled with irony. Did he mean medically, or the ship? Gray pointed at another of the wooden doors. The shape of a pool table had been engraved on the gold plate. "This is the game room. Pool, snooker, card tables, the latest video games, that sort of thing."

As they proceeded down the hallway, they were shown the dining room, library, business center, and small lounge with a dark bar in the rear.

"Should I call ahead?" Lymon asked as he eyed the empty room.

"If you'd like. We can have her favorite beverage waiting, assuming the medical people clear it." Gray pointed to one of the cameras. "Otherwise feel free to just drop in. We monitor constantly, so we'll know immediately and have someone coming on the run."

"I'll bet you don't get much business from the ACLU," Sid observed matter-of-factly.

Gray laughed. "Mr. Harness, we're not a public institution. This is a private and very professional clinic. We treat people's privacy with the utmost care. Believe me, we take our responsibilities for their security and safety most seriously. Your principal is spending a small fortune to come here for a procedure. We will make sure that she is satisfied."

"Yeah, right," Lymon said woodenly.

At Gray's curious look, he added, "Mr. Gray, don't misunderstand. The lady's my principal, and I'm a professional. But then, so are you, so let me give you a heads-up. A courtesy, if you will, from one pro to another. Let's just say that Ms. Weaver is a little, um, flighty. She's not one to stick things out, if you know what I mean. She changes her mind at the last minute. A lot." He glanced at Sid. "What do you think? Fifty-fifty?"

Sid shrugged. "Maybe."

"Meaning?" Gray asked.

"Meaning that we might get a call from Ms. Weaver in the middle of the night tonight or tomorrow morning *demanding* that we get her out of here." Lymon shrugged. "It's our job. What we're paid for. If she decides at the last instant that she doesn't want to go through with this procedure of hers, what's the drill?"

Gray frowned, lips pursed. "If she doesn't, it will complicate things. A lot of people have gone to a lot of trouble to set this up."

Lymon glanced away, lowering his voice. "The people who run her trust are used to, shall we say, 'situations.' My job is to see that we accede to her demands. If we need a helicopter, can we get one?"

"It'll be expensive."

Lymon laughed. "Trust me. She can afford it."

"If we can't use the helicopter that's currently aboard, I'll be able to summon one from the mainland. It might take as much as a couple of hours, or she could go by means of one of the ship's launches, if necessary."

"Thanks. That's good to know."

"What's down there?" Sid asked as they passed a stairway leading down. A substantial steel grating barred passage. It reminded Lymon of one of the scarier scenes in the movie *Titanic.*

"That leads to the lower decks." Gray turned, a fist in his palm. "Gentlemen, your access is restricted to B Deck. If you wish to visit other areas of the ship, please don't hesitate to call my office and a guide will be assigned. We are happy to accommodate visits to places like the engine room, the bridge, and galley. Because of the sensitive and *private* nature of our work, some portions of the ship are off-limits to unauthorized personnel."

Gray forced a smile. "We have had people in the past who, for reasons of their own, tried to break our security. It is our standing rule that anyone who does so will be confined and removed from this vessel at first opportunity. Am I understood?"

"Fair enough," Lymon replied easily.

At the end of the corridor, Gray opened the ornate double doors and led them out onto an open deck surrounded by white steel railings. A large pool surrounded by lounge chairs and tables dominated the center. Another bar was covered by the overhang to the right of the doors. A healthy-looking man and an attractive brunette woman were lounging in a small whirlpool to one side. They looked up, smiled, and waved.

"More clients?"

"Yes. Leaving tomorrow, actually. Traveled down from Canada with us." Gray pointed overhead. "Up the steps you will find the tennis courts."

He indicated the signs at each of the companionways. Arrows pointing downward with a picture of a small-cabined boat. "Follow the signs down to the lifeboats. In an emergency, your assigned lifeboat is A 16. But as a guest, any boat you reach will take you. Peter will have already shown you where flotation devices are located in your room closets. These large cabinets to either side contain others in case we have to evacuate when you're away from the room."

"What about the other guests?" Sid asked.

"We'd like a list if we could," Lymon added. "It

would give us an opportunity to interface with their security, let them know who we are and vice versa."

"As of this moment, you are the only party aboard with security." Gray gave him a sharp look. "As I said, we take our clients' needs and safety very seriously. There are currently no persons aboard who could be considered threats to your principal. Given our monitoring, we will be on top of it in an instant if there is."

"Sounds good." Lymon looked around, seeing nothing but empty ocean beyond. It wasn't a new vista. He and Sid had spent weeks looking out at water from ships in the Persian Gulf. The afternoon sky had taken on a brassy look.

"Is this your first time on a ship?" Gray asked, reading his expression.

"Not hardly."

Gray's beeper went off, and he lifted a small radio from his belt, flipping it open. "Yes?"

"Sir, when you can, we need you in the barn. There's a situation you should be aware of."

"On my way." Gray re-holstered his radio. "Gentlemen, if you need anything, dial the operator. I, or one of my staff, will be back to you immediately." He gave a brief nod. "And thanks for the heads-up on your principal. I'll make sure the proper people are notified in case she changes her mind." He looked back and forth between them. "Anything else?"

"Not at the moment."

"Then, if you will excuse me, I'll get back to the grind."

Gray shook hands again and disappeared through the double doors into the hallway.

"What do you make of that?" Sid asked.

"Top of the line, right down to the helicopter. You think he recognized me?"

"Who?" Then Sid made a chopping gesture, warning in his dark eyes. "Hold that thought and follow me."

Sid led the way to the railing farthest from the bathing couple. As they faced out at the ocean, where swells were shining in the late-afternoon sun, Sid said between gritted teeth, "The room's bugged. We're under a fucking microscope."

"You sure?" Lymon looked down at the water rippling along the steel hull so far below.

"Yeah, I found what I think is a Super Vanguard Sciax 6.5 system in both Jennifer's room and ours. The thing uses top-of-the-line fiberoptics, microlensing, and computer-enhanced resolution, as well as superb directional audio capability. You can hear someone digesting a pizza from across the room. We considered it for surveillance, but it got axed in the budget. Absolutely incredible what it will do. Hell, for all I know, they've got a long-range microphone on us now. Be careful, Lymon. Tell Jennifer to be careful."

"Right."

Sid shook his head. "You and your crime scene. Shit. You can't pass a fart in this place without someone knowing." A pause. "What were you going to say back there?"

"You recognize Gray?"

"Should I?"

"You've seen his picture. LA, at Christal's apartment the night she got grabbed."

Sid's face hardened. "He didn't place you?"

"Not that I could see. If he did, he was better at hiding it than I would have been."

"Think Christal's here?"

"Got me." Lymon frowned down at the shifting waters. "But with this kind of security, I don't think they're going to let us go poking around looking for her."

"Shit! We gotta get the hell out of here."

"Yeah, let's just hope that helicopter is ready when Jennifer throws her fit."

"Amen." Sid looked at him. "Lymon, if your friend Gray wanted to keep us here, what could we do about it?"

"Got me. Whatever it is that we'd have do, it wouldn't be pretty."

"Whu-up!" Sid answered in military slang.

CHAPTER 18

At the knock on the door, Sheela was surprised to find Mary Abernathy standing there. Something seemed to have changed. The woman studied Sheela with a strange new intensity as if seeing her for the first time. "May I come in?"

Sheela wore her shy Jennifer smile and nodded, stepping back.

Abernathy entered with the self-assurance of an M1 battle tank. In a clipped voice, she said, "Our Mr. Gray is providing orientation for your security. I thought we should have a little chat."

As Abernathy took a seat, Sheela settled herself on the overstuffed chair just opposite her. "Okay."

"How are your quarters here?" Where did the hostile tone in her voice come from?

"Just fine. I was expecting, oh, I don't know. Like hammocks and little round portholes. Not like a real hotel."

"Had anything to eat?"

"No. And I'm starved."

Abernathy leaned forward, her smile oddly forced. "Outside of starvation, how are you feeling?"

Sheela took a moment to fidget, then let her glance slide sideways. "I'm fine."

"You're sure?"

Sheela managed a trite Jennifer nod. "Who were the pregnant women? You know, this morning on the launch...there were two pregnant women."

Abernathy hesitated. "Not all of our clients are young and healthy like you are. And some, believe it or not, are actually male. For a fee Genesis Athena will provide a surrogate mother. It's expensive, but for many people it's the only option."

"I see." She made it plain that she didn't.

"All right." Abernathy pressed her hands together. "What if you're a single father and your son dies suddenly? What if that bereaved man feels like you do, Jennifer? Or a gay or transgender couple? What if you want another child? What if someone wants a *specific* child? Should we deny him or her or them when we can help?"

"Well, I, uh—"

"No!" Abernathy waved it away as if it were an irritation. "And it's not just men and LGBTQ people. We know of women, who for reasons of age, or biology, cannot have children. Maybe they've had cancer or had a hysterectomy. Perhaps they're female corporate executives who can't take time out for a pregnancy. Do we deny them but only help people like the Smith couple you met this morning?"

"Well, I don't know."

Abernathy leaned back, one eyebrow lifted. "Jennifer, do you believe in equality?"

"Sure."

"Then why is it, when it comes to reproductive biology, only some people are allowed to reproduce and others aren't?"

Sheela frowned, actually disturbed by the way Mary Abernathy had phrased the question. "It's not a matter of being allowed, is it?"

"Can a man have a child without a female partner?"

"No."

"Is it right?"

"Well…it's how God made us."

"Ah! Of course. God. But, Jennifer, we've been interfering with the way God made us for centuries now. In most cases a baby born prematurely will die without medical intervention. With modern technology, we can save it, and it will grow up to have a normal and happy life. Or would you let it die?"

"Of course I'd save it."

"What if it has a perforated septum in its heart? What's your choice? Do you operate to save it, or let it die?"

"Operate."

"But that's interfering with the way God made that baby."

"But reproducing is different, isn't it?"

"Why? People change gender all the time, now. In the past, our hypothetical baby would have died because we couldn't do anything to save it. We didn't have the technology. Until now, a man couldn't reproduce himself. Genesis Athena makes that possible. If we can provide our service to you, why can't we provide the same service for others in need? The end result is the same: You, or he, or they will have a healthy baby to raise, to be your child. You have a right to a family, Jennifer. Why doesn't everyone?"

She put a hand to her mouth. "I guess..."

"It's a matter of essential equality. At Genesis Athena, we're leveling the playing field for the first time in human history."

Sheela sat back. "So, it's all just a matter of technology? Of tools and science? You're saying that because we can, we should?"

Abernathy smiled kindly. "What you're asking is: Where do you draw the line? But then, that's not the real issue, is it? The question should be, Why should you draw a line at all?"

Sheela frowned. "I guess, since I'm here, I'm not the one to ask that."

"Good." Mary stood. "Are you settled?"

Sheela nodded, looking around. "I'm unpacked. And, well, I don't know. All of a sudden, I'm kind of—"

"A little scared?" Abernathy asked as if she knew full well what Jennifer was going to answer.

"I guess."

"Come on. Let's go for a short walk. I want to show you something and introduce you to some people you'll be working with."

Sheela hesitated. On the one hand, she wanted Lymon close by. On the other, if, as she suspected, they were going to do the usual doctor-patient chat where everything was explained in detail, it would give her the excuse she needed to back out.

"Will it take long?"

"Barring complications, half an hour, if that. We'll treat you to a marvelous dinner when we're finished."

Sheela seemed to mull it over. "Sure. Let me contact

Lymon so he doesn't tear the ship apart looking for me."

"Use the phone." Abernathy pointed. "He'll find the voice message when he and Mr. Gray return from their tour."

Sheela gave the woman her insecure Jennifer smile and reached for the phone. After leaving a message for Lymon, she followed Abernathy out into the corridor and to the right, where one of the elevators waited, doors open.

Sheela stepped inside. She watched Abernathy press the button for H Deck. "You're going to like the people who will be working with you. We've found that if instead of waiting out the first night alone, you socialize with the staff, you'll feel better about the procedure."

"I see."

Abernathy studied her thoughtfully as the lift slowed, dinged, and the door opened. "We've also determined from the blood sample I took in New York that our window is very narrow."

Sheela followed her out into a white corridor. "What window is that?"

"A most curious biological one. This way."

Two men in white uniforms, both darkly complected, stepped out, nodding at Mary Abernathy. They dropped in behind Sheela as Mary started off down the hall.

Sheela glanced nervously at the men hovering behind, wondering if Jennifer should say anything, or just take this in stride.

Abernathy seemed brusque, oddly tense. Or was it

just that things had happened so fast? She hadn't had time to just sit and think, to put the plan in order.

Abernathy stopped before a door marked EXAMINATION and opened it. "If you'd step inside, Jennifer."

Sheela entered to find a wood-veneer-paneled waiting room with comfortable couches, a coffee table, and magazines. Soft music drifted down from the speakers. It could have been lifted from any doctor's office in the country.

Abernathy gave a signal to the two men, who remained outside, and closed the door. "The nice thing"—Abernathy gestured Sheela to follow her—"is that we don't have to wait. Come on. We're all set."

"For what?" Sheela asked as she stepped into a hallway and was led down to a small room. Here, what looked like a dentist's chair dominated a small examining room. The noxious odors of medical chemicals stung her nose.

"Take a seat," Abernathy told her. "It's the most comfortable one in the house." She made a face. "Oh, don't worry. We just need to take a blood sample. Simple really. It has to be done while you've got an empty stomach. As soon as we do the vampire thing, we'll be off for dinner with our specialists so that you have a chance to relax."

As Sheela uncertainly settled into the seat, an attractive young woman of either Middle Eastern or Indian descent entered. She was perhaps thirty, with high cheeks and sleek black hair pulled back and clipped. Her white uniform was slightly baggy, somewhat Oriental in style. "Hello, Ms. Weaver. I'm Asza. This will only take a moment." She walked up and smiled down at Sheela in a reassuring manner. "You'll barely feel a thing."

Sheela glanced down at the syringe in the woman's hand. "Uh, I don't know if I want to—"

"Shhh!" Abernathy put a playful finger to her lips. "It's just a hormone to prepare your system. Trust me, it won't hurt a bit. It won't affect you at all. Well, sometimes women have minor hot flashes the next day, but that's about it."

"Wait!" Sheela said as Asza leaned down and swabbed her arm with alcohol. "I'm not ready for this!"

"The empty stomach," Abernathy said, leaning down and insisting. "It's very important. And then, in a shake, we're off to dinner. I think you'll enjoy it. We've got a baked halibut that's marinated in—"

Asza slipped the sharp needle into Sheela's arm. She watched in horror as the plunger injected a clear fluid into her vein.

CHAPTER 19

Hank and April bent over the small table studying their latest assignment: obtaining a sample from George Clooney. The actor was currently shooting a film in New York. Hank and April had been perusing the street maps, comparing them with the locations the production company had filed for with the New York film commission, and trying to decipher the security at the New York Four Seasons Hotel.

"There are a million ways to do this. It's DNA, for God's sake!"

"It has to be high profile," April insisted. "People have to *know* that we've got the real thing."

April's phone buzzed and she pulled it from a pocket. Listened, and said, "We've got to go. Security center. Now."

"What's up?"

"Security alert. Something big's coming down."

Next thing they were in the hall, Hank following on her heels. He liked hurrying along behind April. The view from the rear was delightful. And to hell with those who'd condemn him for "male gaze."

Their route took them up two decks and down a long central passageway. A large metal hatch was marked SECURITY CENTER. April ran her fingers over a numeric keypad, then spun the wheel.

"We've got a problem," Neal told them as they entered. He stood in front of a bank of glowing monitors in the security center. Each screen showed different parts of the ship. The feed from each camera was monitored by the central computer. As long as no movement was detected, the computer ignored that image. It was a neat system, smart, and helped avoid errors that came from boredom on the operator's part.

For the moment, the single large screen in the center of the complex displayed an attractive woman reclining in a chair as white-dressed nurses scurried about her, hooking up monitors, IVs, and other assorted medical apparatus.

Hank and April slid in behind the two work tables with five of the other security guys.

"I wanted you two since you've both had experience with Sheela Marks." Neal was looking back and forth between April and Hank.

"What?" April asked, straightening in her chair. "That was weeks ago."

"Who is that, April?" Neal pointed to where one of the nurses peeled a brunette wig from a tightly coiffed red-blond head. Hank could see another of the nurses teasing brown contacts from a glassy blue eye.

"Shit!" April spat. "How'd she get here?"

"She slipped right past us." Neal crossed his arms. "She's registered as Jennifer Weaver, come to have a procedure. I just got a call from my source in California with a heads-up that she might be headed our way."

"What would she want with us?" April asked, a frown deepening between her delicate brows.

"Better yet," Neal asked, "what are we going to do with her?"

For a moment the room was silent, expressions grim. Hank could understand the dilemma. This wasn't a mere blip on the radar. Not a Crystal Anaya who could disappear if necessary. If they deep-sixed Sheela Marks, someone *would* come looking.

"Jennifer Weaver." Neal glanced up from a sheaf of notes he'd picked up. "Apparently one of her screen characters."

Hank remembered: the saucy if insecure vixen from *Joy's Girl.*

"Her attorney—Felix Baylor, a big gun in the LA legal world, set up an account for her alias and paid down a pretty big deposit." Neal glanced from one to the other. "A lot of firepower could be leveled at us if this isn't handled just right."

"How did you tag her?" Hank asked.

"We might even have missed her despite the tip, but apparently the woman knows more about acting than she does about genetics. She asked for implantation of one of her own clones."

April burst out laughing.

"What's the joke?" Hank asked from the side of his mouth.

"They'd chart identically in the lab. Like a crook submitting his own fingerprint when he volunteered to help solve his own crime."

"Got it." Hank frowned.

"So, people, what do we do?" Neal gestured at the screen. "She doesn't know we're onto her. She's under sedation and out of trouble while we figure out how to handle this thing."

"I say she has an accident," one of the shipboard guys said. "Maybe the launch has a little bad luck? An explosion just before she and her party docks at the pier in Brooklyn?"

"No way," Hank countered. "The launch is already under Coast Guard scrutiny. Right now they know that something's going on under their nose. The first time I was here, I was stopped by them. Believe me, they know that high-profile people are traveling out here, and maybe even have a hint at what we're doing. But until they get a flag, they're not going to show up to do a 'safety inspection' and search of the ship."

Neal nodded. "For the time being, they know we carry enough senators, judges, and congressmen out here to cut us a little slack. Hank's right. Let's not make more trouble for ourselves that way."

"What about the Anaya option?" Hank asked.

All eyes turned his way.

Hank spread his hands. "We were going to drop Anaya in Kingston, Jamaica, stoned on good dope, and let her wake up in the local pokey. The cover was that she ditched her friends back in California for a drug binge. It gives us deniability when and if she tries to finger us for jacking her."

April gave him a thoughtful look. "You mean just substitute Sheela Marks? What about the law firm? This Felix character? He'd know."

"What would he know?" Hank shot back. "With the right spin, we could say that Marks did this sort of thing on occasion, always with a well-rehearsed alibi for being where she was not. She might have scheduled an elective 'medical' procedure with Genesis Athena, but at the last minute, booked a flight from New York to Kingston as Jennifer Weaver to let her hair down out of the spotlight."

Neal had listened with pursed lips. "You think you could put that together and make it stick?"

"Yeah." Hank leaned back. "It would take a little setup, but it could be done." He glanced at April. "You've got a little darker hair, gray instead of blue eyes, but with the right makeup, you could pass for her. We could fly down on the first available flight, score some drugs, throw some wild parties, and book it all to Weaver's credit card. We sneak Marks in, tailor a drug cocktail, and call the hospital to report an OD on our way out of town."

April was nodding, putting it together in her mind. He could see the quickening of anticipation in her eyes. "Damn, I'll miss getting a piece of George Clooney. He's supposed to have such a way with women."

"One hitch," Neal replied. "What about Marks' security?"

"Piece of cake," April said. "We got by those guys twice. Once in New York, once in LA, so we can do it again."

"And almost got nicked," Neal added. "Both times."

Hank tensed, remembering the hard-eyed look Lymon Bridges had given him in the LBA offices that day.

"That second time was Anaya," April replied. "And if you'll recall, she's belowdecks."

"Who's with Marks?" Hank asked. "Show me."

Neal turned to the bearded man sitting at the monitor control panel. "Vince? Could you give me a visual of the Weaver security detail?"

Within seconds the monitor changed, Sheela Marks vanishing to be replaced by a shot of Lymon Bridges prowling down the B Deck corridor. He walked in easy strides, like a muscular predator. Behind him, a thickset man followed a half-step behind, arms swinging slowly. Hank stood, rounding the table to stare. "I don't fucking believe it!"

"What?" April and Neal asked in unison.

"People, take a close look. That's Special Agent Sid Harness of the Washington Metro Field Office. FBI."

"You're sure?" Neal asked, coming to stand beside him.

"Yeah. Real sure." Hank took a deep breath. "Game time, folks. The feds are here. Things just got a whole lot trickier."

"So, what do we do?" Neal asked.

Hank chewed on his lip as he thought. "Let me make some calls. I might have an idea."

CHAPTER 20

The cramped bathroom was in quarters belonging to a female nurse named Asza, whereabouts currently unknown. Christal stepped in to straddle the toilet as Brian closed the door behind them. A white technician's uniform hung from a hook behind the door. It looked clean, crisp, and freshly pressed.

Brian gave her a grin, that sexy twinkle in his eyes. His Australian accent seemed to have thickened in the close quarters. "You see, the thing is, Asza is one of the Sheik's nieces. He wouldn't dare allow a camera to monitor her during her private moments. And, fortunately for us, she never locks her quarters."

"Brian? How did Nancy Hartlee get out of here?"

The twinkle died. "She was involved with one of the guards at the controlled entry. She worked on it for a long time. You know, just going for casual conversations. After a couple of months, he started sneaking in, spending the nights in her quarters. No one gave it much thought. Just two people having an affair."

"So, what happened?"

"One night she came to me. Brought me here." Pain reflected in Brian's eyes. "She said she was going up top, that she'd talked the guy into letting her see the stars. He took her out. Got her past the security somehow. It was like camel crap hitting the road the next morning when Nancy didn't show up for work. The guards were replaced by Max and Hans—the two gay guys—and we didn't hear another word about Nancy until you confirmed her body was identified."

Christal felt her guts drop. "Damn, I thought maybe it was through some vent or something."

"Sorry." He seemed to be musing. "You know, over the years, almost everything's been tried at least once. That's why most of the staff's been replaced with trained members of the Sheik's family."

"Security-friendly."

"What's this thing with Jennifer Weaver?"

She took his hand, reassured just to touch him. "I work for her. Or, I should say my company does. Jennifer Weaver is Sheela Marks. Weaver was her breakout role. She must have gotten her hands on the information I've compiled about Genesis Athena. At least, that's my guess. Just shooting from the hip, I'd say she set up an appointment for one of your cloning procedures, figuring she'd come right to the source and find out what it was all about. She's probably got my boss and some of his people following in tow." She gave him a wicked grin. "Brian, if there was ever a time to get the hell out of Dodge, this is it."

"Where's Dodge?"

"It's a bit north of Alice Springs."

"Christal, I don't wish to rain on your parade here,

but how are you planning to get past the controlled entrance? You saw that, right? How it works? And then there are the security cameras in the hallways. It's a bleeding fortress, and you're smack in the center of it."

"Uh, you don't have a couple of Arnold Schwarzenegger clones hanging around, do you? Maybe with a couple of M79 grenade launchers?"

"Sorry. We don't do Terminators here."

"How about Linda Hamilton?"

"I'm afraid not. At least we haven't seen her sample come through yet."

"She did pretty well with just a paper clip."

"I don't follow."

"Wait a minute." She tilted her head, weaving her fingers into his. "McEwan can come and go as he wants, right?"

"Forget it, he's *not* going to sign you a pass. He's the biggest prick on the boat. No way he'll take a fall...and you can't bribe him."

"Who's his superior?"

"No one. He reports straight to the Sheik. He's the head of the biological section."

"So, he can do anything he wants, anytime?"

"Pretty much. Like I say, he's thick with them."

"You know him, Brian. If it came down to him or Genesis Athena, what would he do?"

"He'd save his neck."

She was thinking hard on that, aware suddenly that he was staring at her mouth. "What?"

"Do you know that you stick your tongue out of the corner of your mouth when you're concentrating?"

"I've heard that before."

He reached out, running his other hand down her

sleek hair. "I'd love to tell you that McEwan had a weakness other than his vanity. Dickless shit that he is, he acts like he sits immediately to the right of God's throne. To hear him tell it, he *is* Genesis Athena, and the world has yet to understand how great he is."

It began to click in Christal's mind. "Brian? How desperate are you?"

"Desperate enough to take their buyout. Desperate enough to take a chance on you."

"You mean that?" And oddly, his answer was important to her.

"God help me, I don't think I could stay here now. I'd give the world for a chance to get to know you."

"I don't need the world, Brian." She reached up and took his other hand in hers. "Just a little help from you and a bit of courage."

"What? About taking their buyout?"

She shook her head. "McEwan knows that Sheela's aboard. Copperhead—your April Hayes—knows that I work for her. They're putting the pieces together as we speak, so we've got to move fast."

"It's going to be dangerous, isn't it?"

Christal nodded.

He smiled shyly at her. "Whatever it takes, I'm here for you."

She slid her arms around his neck, pulling him to her. His lips met hers gently, and she turned into his kiss. Her heart began to beat, and her breasts felt sensitive as they brushed his chest. She let her memory linger on the dashing light that sometimes filled his eyes, and how those lips on hers bent into that devilish smile.

Finally, she leaned back, sighing. "I could get to like that."

"Me, too," he whispered. "Now, just what do you have in mind?"

"Hand me that uniform hanging on the door. If I'm not mistaken, Asza is about my size."

CHAPTER 21

"This is bullshit," Lymon growled as he knocked on Sheela's suite door. "She wouldn't have charged off and left a trite little phone message on the machine." He rattled the handle, finding it locked.

"It sounded like a prissy little girl," Sid reminded him as he watched up and down the corridor. "Lymon, what do you really know about her?"

"Enough." He shot a hard glare at Sid.

"Yeah, so?"

"So"—he lowered his voice—"someone was there, with her, when she left that message."

In an equally rough whisper, Sid replied, "She might have been playing to the audience: you. Come on, Lymon. She ditched you in LA so she could come here. Maybe she's doing just what she wants to."

Lymon glared, voice hoarse. "You mean that? Or are you playing to the audience, too?" He jerked his head toward the closest security camera.

Sid shrugged. "You tell me."

"I *know* the lady."

"You're in love with her. That's different."

"Shut up, Sid." Lymon turned on his heel, striding down to their door; a building panic was fueled by anger in his gut. They hadn't even had a chance to get their stories straight, and poof! She was gone. Vanished into the bowels of the *ZoeGen.*

"If they figure this out," Sid muttered as he leaned close, "she'd make one hell of a hostage."

"I said, shut up." Lymon crossed his suite in long steps and picked up the phone, dialing zero. At the voice, he said, "This Lymon Bridges, Ms. Weaver's security. Give me Neal Gray, please."

"One moment."

The moment lasted three long minutes, during which Lymon's desperation quotient got jacked up another couple of notches.

A voice said, *"This is Vince Harmon. I'm sorry, Mr. Gray isn't available. May I be of assistance?"*

"I need to know the location of Ms. Weaver."

"One moment." A slight pause. *"She's currently in conference with our counselors."*

"Can you put me through? I need to speak with her."

"I'm sorry, sir. She can't be interrupted. I'll contact our floor security and make sure that she is notified of your call as soon as she's out of her session."

"No, Vince. You'll put me through right now." He tried to keep his voice flat and emotionless. From Sid's expression, it didn't work.

"I'm sorry, sir. The counseling conference cannot be interrupted. I will have her call you the moment she's finished. That's the best I can do."

"Hey, pal! It's not good enough!"

Sid was shaking his head in warning.

"Make sure she calls!" Lymon bellowed before he hung up. "What?"

"What are you going to do? Charge forth, beating down doors until you find her? You know the score here. You're a smart guy, Lymon. Do you really think you can get off this deck without Gray's goons mobbing you and bundling your butt back here? You're not thinking." A pause. "It's not like you."

"No, I suppose not."

Someone had once told him that human beings were just oversophisticated chimpanzees. He considered that as he stepped away from the phone instead of ripping it out of the wall and throwing it. "What's the look for?"

Sid's face had softened. "I hope she's worth it. That's all."

"Worth what?"

"All the love you have for her."

"Yeah, well, sometimes, Sid, it ain't all it's cracked up to be." Lymon started for the door. "I can't just sit here like a bug in a jar. I need to figure out how to get into my tactical case; then we're going out."

"We going to get into trouble?"

"What do you think?"

CHAPTER 22

At his chair in the security center, Vince Harmon watched Lymon Bridges as he walked into the bedroom, threw his black plastic case on the bed, and then pulled the cover over himself. The other guy, the one he'd been told was FBI, yawned and stretched.

Vince changed the camera angle, switching from one fiber-optic lens to the next. No matter how good the system, he couldn't see through the bedspread.

Report it?

Even as he considered, Bridges threw the spread back, made a negative gesture to Harness, and stalked out of the room, his suit coat neat and a determined look on his face.

Vince played with his controls, flashing back to the bed. The case sat half-exposed, still locked.

"Come on," Vince whispered. "Give it a try. You can't beat our system, asshole."

CHAPTER 23

Gregor stepped out of the Sheik's opulent suite on A Deck and closed the door behind him. He nodded to the two security guards who stood outside; sinister-looking black machine guns hung from straps at their shoulders. The guns came as a surprise. That was a new twist, but then, this was a curious new development: the first infiltration by an outsider that they were aware of.

Gregor straightened his smock and walked to the lift that would take him from the Sheik's palatial quarters down into the bowels of the ship. He pressed the button and waited until the doors slipped open.

Inside the lift, he thumbed the button and watched the lights flicker until the lift stopped on H Deck. Stepping out, he padded past doorways down the illuminated white hall; the passing staff nodded politely, often giving him faint smiles.

He shouldn't be bursting with this sort of excitement, but he felt absolutely exhilarated. They had known that someday they would be faced with this situation. Gregor was actually amazed that it had taken this long before someone finally wised up.

"Everything in its time," the Sheik had said calmly, his dark eyes glowing. "This, my dear Gregor, is our time."

"What are we going to do?" he had asked.

The Sheik had steepled his long brown fingers, smiled, and replied, "Let it play out as it is meant to, Doctor."

Gregor smacked a fist into his palm as he found the right door, flashed his implanted wrist over the lock plate, and entered. He walked up to a glass partition and was raising his hand to the intercom when his personal com buzzed in his pocket.

Pulling it out, he flipped it open and accessed his personal channel. Brian Everly was staring out at him with worried eyes. "Gregor? Do you have a minute? Something's come up."

"Such as?"

"An irregularity."

"Brian, I'm right in the middle of something."

Everly gave him that old familiar "You're an idiot" look that had grated on Gregor's nerves from the moment they'd met.

"What is it?"

"Something that you apparently missed on Sheela Marks' chromosome six. But, what the hell, what are a couple of spare nucleotides? It's probably nothing, right, mate?"

"Where are you?"

"Lab six."

“Be right there.” Brian flipped his PDA closed, gave one last look through the window, and headed for the door.

“Asshole Aussie! Who does he think he is? Crocodile Dundee?”

CHAPTER 24

Past the tennis courts on B Deck, Lymon led them to a blank wall. The steel here had been painted white, but he could see where all the windows but one had been welded over with steel plate. An armed guard stood before the only door, a serious-looking hatch with a sophisticated lock plate and numerical pad. The guard was a big guy, and he held a Heckler & Koch MP5 sub gun in both hands. His smoky dark-brown eyes seemed to say "Try me" as he watched Lymon and Sid approach. He spoke softly into a collar mic, the sibilant Arabic barely audible.

"What now, boss?" Sid asked, eyeing the guy.

"We smile...and try something else." Lymon did just that, trying to act nonchalant as he stared around, noting the cameras and the two stairways that led to the roof. Both were closed off with the metal-grated doors. Above, just visible over the lip of the roof, was the unmistakable protrusion of a helicopter blade.

"Looks to me like that's our ride out of here." Lymon gave the slightest nod, but Sid had already picked it up. "Yeah, assuming we can get someone to fly the thing."

"You still tuned up from our stint in the Marines?" Lymon turned, leading the way back past the tennis courts.

"Hey," Sid answered. "That was for five minutes, with a real pilot in the left seat covering for any screwups. We don't even know what kind of machine that is up there. I'd kill us faster in that helicopter than that goon back there would with that sub gun."

"Just a thought." Lymon led the way down the stairs to the B Deck. This time it was empty, the bathing couple having gone in. The dining room had been occupied as they went out. Supper time. Lymon's belly kept reminding him.

"How's your ability with locks?"

"Damn good, as you well know."

"That was a handy little skill you picked up. Saved our asses a couple of times, if you'll recall. Not to mention the advantages it gave us in getting into the AAFES warehouse at Camp Bondsteel."

"We damn near got hung over that, too."

"Yeah, but we didn't." Lymon stopped by the pool, picking up one of the sections of aluminum rod from the cleaning accessories. "Let's see how far we get."

"We're gonna regret this."

"There's only one camera that points at the grating leading down to C Deck." Lymon ran the pole back and forth in his hands. "The lock looked like a simple one. If I jar that camera just a bit out of alignment..."

"I hope Claire's satisfied with my life insurance and pension."

"I guess she'll have to be, huh?"

CHAPTER 25

On two different occasions in the post-9/11 world, Christal had run headlong into racial discrimination. The first time was in December of 2015 when she was asked to deplane from a commuter flight taking her from DIA in Denver to Albuquerque. The pilot, a guy with a Massachusetts accent, had said he was uncomfortable with her aboard. Only her FBI credentials and the assent of the other passengers, most of them locals who knew what Latinos looked like, had allowed her to remain on board.

The second time had been in Charlotte, North Carolina, a couple of months later, when she was singled out and taken into a back room, where a female TSA officer had had her undress while her luggage was dismantled piece by piece because she looked "suspicious." That time they had tried to take her FBI shield and folder to see if it had been "reproduced."

A call to the Charlotte Field Office—where she'd been visiting—finally got her off the hook to fly, fuming, back to DC. Now, for the first time, she could actually use her dark complexion to her advantage. If all those screeners could be wrong, so, too, might the *ZoeGen* security guy, Hans.

Assuming this doesn't just get me killed.

But then, if she was going to get the hell out, risks had to be taken. God knew, Sheela was taking one hell of a chance just setting foot on the *ZoeGen.*

The white uniform fit a little tighter than Christal would have liked. It hugged her hips and breasts a little too snugly for comfort. Nevertheless, she had followed Brian Everly to one of the labs and now stood slightly behind where he sat peering into a microscope. She tried to look like she was jotting notes in a folder he had given her.

Surreptitiously, she glanced from the corner of her eye, seeing the camera that clung to the corner of the ceiling like a malevolent gremlin. The bulge in her skirt pocket was unsettling, as much for what it was as for what it represented.

Am I going to be able to do this?

God, it was one thing to think about the plan, to rehearse it in the mind's eye—but quite another to carry it out.

She took a deep breath, trying to still the pounding of her heart. In the polished surface of a stainless steel autoclave she checked her reflection: white uniform, her dark hair secured modestly behind her neck, and a pinned white technician's hat. A facial mask hung at half-staff, Brian having informed her that it was part of the post-COVID uniform, as were the nitril gloves protruding from her left pocket.

"Where the hell is he?" Brian muttered under his breath.

"It hasn't been but a couple of minutes since you called." She glanced at the clock on the far wall. "Less than two, actually."

He looked up at her, eyes pleading. "Are you sure you want to do this? Wouldn't it be better if it were me?"

"Have you ever had to kill someone, Brian?"

"No." He cocked his head. "Have you?"

She gave a slight shake of the head, keeping her voice low. "But at least I was trained to. And I made the decision long ago that if I ever had to, I would."

"Pray it doesn't come to that, right?"

She screwed her lips up, twisting the pronunciation to something similar to the Australian "Right, mate!"

A second later, the lab door whipped open, and Gregor came striding in. In the quick glance Christal managed before she averted her face, he looked irritated. She concentrated on jotting nonsense in her folder as he crossed the room.

"Very well, Brian. This had better be good. Just what the hell is so damn important? Don't tell me it's some silly point mutation in an alu or something."

"Take a look," Brian said, tension dripping from his voice.

Later, Christal was sure it was nerves rather than acting, that had made it sound so ominous, but Gregor slipped into the chair as Brian made way. Gregor's fingers went to the microscope focus as he rested his forehead against the viewer.

Brian gave Christal a pleading look as she reached into her pocket and removed the syringe. In answer she shot him a reassuring smile and stepped beside Gregor McEwan where he peered into the hooded microscope. "I don't see a bloody damned—"

Christal leaned down and jabbed the needle into his side just above the hip bone, saying, "Stand up, Gregor, and don't make a fucking move, or I'll squirt this shit right inside you."

He froze, face still pressed against the viewer. "What the hell?"

"I said, stand up, and do it slowly. We wrapped elastic around the plunger. That means if you twist away, the plunger drops. You get it?"

Gregor carefully pulled his head back, raising his eyes to meet Christal's. "Whatever you think you're doing, it's not going to work."

"It's worked before," Brian said too quickly. "It's your invention, after all. I filled the syringe with five ccs of your CAT delivery system. The one you developed for the psychologists."

Gregor stiffened. "*Five* ccs! You idiot, that would kill me!"

"Yes, quite," Brian continued. "And in a most unpleasant way."

"What's it do?" Christal asked. "You didn't have time to fill me in on all the details."

"A small virus delivers a ribosomal RNA strand that inhibits the production of acetylcholine in the nerve cells. Without ACh, as it's called, the nerves cease to function. Gregor's dosage was infinitesimal, measured in microliters. It was just enough to put the brakes on choline acetyltransferase, or CAT, in people with over-active production."

"Right." Christal nodded. "Whatever you said."

"What do you want?" Gregor asked, smart enough to get with the program.

Christal leaned close, whispering, "I want you to stand up. As you do, you're going to put your arm around my waist. You know, just like I was your girlfriend. Get the picture? Then you and I are going to walk out of here, smiling and laughing like the old friends we are. After we're past the security door, you're going to take us to Sheela Marks' quarters. When we get there, we'll give you further instructions."

Gregor closed his eyes, body stiff. She could almost hear his brain running through alternate endings to his current dilemma.

"Come on, Gregor," she told him gently. "We're standing up now. If you don't come when I lift you, this plunger might drop a little. You know, from the awkward position and all."

He came, rising slowly, gently, letting Christal wind her arm around his side. Brian, perspiration beading on his pale skin, took a moment to place a small towel over the offending needle so that it appeared to be draped over Christal's arm.

"You know, just a few microliters will cause me serious physiological damage, Brian."

"Oh, yes. I'm quite aware." Brian rubbed his hands together nervously. "I'm sure you're worried about seepage from the large-gauge needle, but we took the precaution of placing a small wax plug in the channel. Not much—just enough to ensure that if you cooperate, you'll be able to enjoy a long and prosperous future."

Gregor took a deep breath. Christal could feel the fear radiating out of him. Could almost smell it, sour and acidic. When he looked down, he could see the elastic-wrapped syringe protruding from just above his hip.

"Put your arm around me," she insisted. "Do it slowly, gently." She gave him a smile. "You were interested in me once, Gregor. I saw it in your eyes. What happened? Did I lose my charm?"

"You *can't* get off the ship. Neither can Marks and her people. This *isn't* going to work."

"You'd better help us figure out a way to make it work, then," Brian said, gesturing toward the door. "After you. Oh, and when we get to the box, you just tell Max to let us past, and that I'm wanted upstairs, you got that?"

"And if you don't"—Christal placed her lips next to his ear—"the plunger goes down. After that, you're dead, and we make up whatever story we want to."

Gregor stared down at the hidden syringe. "Aye, I get the picture. Let's go. The sooner this is over, the sooner I get that damn thing oot o' me side."

CHAPTER 26

Gregor tried to swallow but couldn't. His mouth had gone dry, and his tongue stuck. With each step, he could feel the sting as the needle shifted in his flesh. Dear God, what if they hadn't really plugged it? Would he begin to malfunction? Would his brain and muscles turn sluggish and then simply shut off?

He shot a glance at Brian. The man looked on the verge of doing something rash. The bunching of his jaw muscles, the fevered quickness of eye—it all bespoke a terrible desperation.

When he got a good look at Anaya's face, he could see a focused determination in the flash of her dark-brown eyes. Why the hell had he ever let her have the run of the deck down here? Of all the stupid mistakes! He almost tripped as panic built inside him.

"Easy," Christal soothed, tightening her arm around his waist. "Don't miss a step. If you fall, this could all go very wrong."

"You have no idea." Sweat was beading on his face

and trickling down from his armpits. What a horrible way to die. Having the nerves just shut off. His brain, his marvelous brain, would go inert, just become a gray-white blob of protein and fat from which no more dreams would be spun. All of it, everything he hadn't written down, would simply cease, locked forever between mute nerves that slowly suffocated in the lonely darkness of isolation.

"Last chance for a check," Brian said as they rounded the corner to the security entrance. "You're sweating, Gregor."

"I'm not the only one."

"Take the towel. Wipe him off." Christal indicated the cloth draped over the syringe.

Brian did, his pale blue eyes reflecting how close he was to panic. His movements were too quick, blocky. "Frightened, Brian?"

"You bet I am. If this goes wrong, we're all fucked, mate."

"You always were a spineless shit," Gregor answered as Brian replaced the towel.

"Yes," Brian admitted, straightening. "I suppose so. But what the hell have I got to lose? You've seen to that, Gregor, so I suppose that you and I have finally come to the end of our little Greek tragedy. So, let's go play it out, shall we?"

"Move it," Anaya said grimly, and her arm propelled Gregor forward. "It's up to you, Greg. The next five minutes are going to determine how you live out your future. Your decision, buddy. Long and happy, or really short and miserable."

He stopped before the lock plate, reaching out with a trembling arm. "I choose long and happy." He pressed the button and leaned awkwardly, carefully, forward for the retinal scan. "Max? It's Gregor, open up."

The door clicked, and Gregor summoned all of his courage to step into the box. He found a grin from somewhere, tightening his hold on Anaya's waist, and looked through the glass. Max was scrutinizing Brian, who looked terribly uncomfortable as he followed them in. He flinched as if at a gunshot when the heavy door clicked shut behind him.

"It's all right, Max," Gregor called. "Brian's wanted upstairs. The Sheik wants to have a little discussion with him."

"Sir?" Max asked, hesitating.

"I authorize it, all right? Don't take all fucking night!" Gregor roared, losing his patience. "I've got things to do!" He indicated Christal, who had her head half averted, as if embarrassed by his attentions.

The door clicked, and Gregor muttered under his breath as they stepped out into the hallway. His legs went suddenly rubbery. Christal's supporting arm tightened reflexively.

"Good work," Christal told him. "You even convinced me."

"Fuck! Right. Thanks for nothing, you mean."

"That's my Gregor," Brian added from behind. "Pissy as an ant, even when he's getting a bleeding compliment. Which way?"

"Down the hall and to the right," Christal said. "There shouldn't be any trouble going the way I went last time, right, Gregor?"

"Right. Whatever."

"Yeah," Christal agreed. "I'd hate like hell to step off

the lift into a mass of gun-toting security guys. It might make me let loose of this plunger."

"I just want this thing out of my side!" Gregor heard the whimper in his voice.

To his relief, the lift was waiting. They walked inside, Christal giving him a curious look. "B Deck?"

"Oddly enough, you're correct."

"The suite with the swimming pool?"

"No. Across the hall."

"Too bad," she answered wryly as Brian pressed the button. "I could get used to that."

To his complete surprise, Gregor had to fight back a smile as the image of Anaya's naked body formed in his mind. She still had no idea of what he'd done to her. Of his little joke. And that knowledge, insignificant as it might seem on the surface, gave him the first tiny ray of hope. He glanced up at the camera in the corner; the glassy round eye was staring down at him with a benevolence he could feel. Was Vince watching him, even now? He stared up at the lens, his mouth moving slowly to form the word "Help!"

It was at that moment that Christal Anaya kissed him full on the lips.

CHAPTER 27

Lymon lifted the aluminum pole and jabbed at the camera. With satisfaction he saw that he'd jimmied it off to one side. He nodded to Sid, who bent over the lock, his picks sliding into the slot. Lymon took a deep breath. God, his hands were sweaty, and his nerves were tingling.

What the hell has happened to you?

In the old days, he'd been wound tight-but-fearless during a mission. He'd lived for that adrenaline high that came with the closing presence of danger. Now his overstretched nerves left him feeling sick and spineless.

To make matters worse, his imagination was playing with him, spinning out images of Sheela. None of them were happy. He remembered the Sheik's fixation that night in New York, that gleam of anticipation in his eyes. He could see Sheela—his Sheela—forced to accede to any perversion. And how would she react? Would her soul retreat, flee back to a shadowed bridge abutment somewhere in Saskatoon?

"Come on, Sid." He couldn't keep the fear out of his voice.

"Just a second. There's only one more tumbler."

That's when it fell apart. Three of them, wearing suits and sunglasses, came in through the double doors. Two more rounded the far corner of the B Deck hallway, striding purposefully forward.

"We're fucked!" Lymon hissed as Sid straightened, palming his lockpicks.

The three Arabs stood shoulder to shoulder; each held an HK MP5, the SD model with a built-in sound suppressor, in the ready position. They stopped no more than five feet away, the first—in accented English —ordered, "Put your hands up, please."

"Hey, wait a minute!" Lymon protested. "We're here with Jennifer Weaver. She's a client. You guys back off, and we'll have Neal Gray straighten this out."

"Sorry, he's busy right now," Hank Abrams said as he strode through the doors behind the three guards.

Lymon shot a glance over his shoulder to see the two blockers firmly in position, weapons at half-mast. Shit!

Abrams walked up behind the suited Arabs, saying, "If you would simply walk down the corridor, gentlemen, we won't have to cause any disturbance. Our other guests are at supper, and it would really piss me off if we upset them."

"Hey, Hank, what's up?" Sid asked.

"Hello, Sid. I'm afraid you're up. Kind of like a sore thumb." He gestured. "Let's move, people. And quietly. If you make a scene, I promise I'll pay you back for it big time. Be good, guys, and maybe we can come to some sort of peaceful resolution, huh?"

"Yeah." Sid turned, hands up, and Lymon followed.

The blockers had moved up to their suite door; one of them opened it and stepped inside. The other took a half-step back, his weapon at the ready.

"Nice work. Who trained these guys?" Sid asked.

"Neal did," Abrams said from the rear. "He doesn't like fuckups. Something you might want to seriously contemplate. Step into your room, please, gentlemen, and do it in a way that won't cause my guy in there to cut you in half with a burst."

"Right." Lymon had that cold sweaty feeling of impending disaster. What the hell were they going to do now? He took a moment to study the guards: Each was alert, his thumb resting on the fire selector. Now wasn't the time to try anything stupid. Lymon walked to the middle of the room, Sid coming to stand beside him.

Hank entered last. He gave them a knowing smile and sadly shook his head. "The second I recognized you, Sid, I just knew you were going to push it." He shifted his attention to Lymon. "And you, Mr. God-almighty Bridges—I feel like I owe you one."

"How's that?"

"For jacking me around in your office that day. You didn't have to do that, you know. You could have just given me Christal's address, and maybe we could have avoided a whole pile of shit."

Sid interjected sourly, "Yeah, a kidnapping with witnesses just isn't the same as a good clean snatch, huh? Forget it, Hank. It's out of control. They got photos of you and Neal that night. Why do you think we're here?"

"Maybe you were in the market for a pleasure

cruise?" Hank gestured to one of his guards. "Pat them down from top to bottom. Turn their pockets inside out and take their belts. Now, Sid, Bridges, if you make this difficult, we can search you just as easily if you're unconscious and bleeding from the scalp."

"You'll fuck up the carpet," Lymon noted as he tapped the thick Persian with his foot.

"Housecleaning has a big steam cleaner." Hank nodded to his goons. "Go."

"You know how the Bureau hates to have one of its own go bad." Sid made a *tsking* sound with his tongue as thorough hands relieved him of the HK Compact and spare magazine. Then his lockpicks, belt, and pockets were "liberated."

Sid continued, "We're after you, buddy. If we'd known you were aboard, the Coast Guard would be swarming this tub from top to bottom trying to sniff you out."

Hank crossed his arms. "So, what are you suggesting? That I just stick my wrists out, let you slap the cuffs on, and go willingly?"

The guards followed suit with Lymon, taking his HK, the flash-bang he'd tucked into an inside pocket, and the portable satellite phone he'd clipped to the back of his belt. Their accumulated possessions were piled onto a towel.

"Take that up to the security center," Hank ordered. "And don't forget the case on the bed in the back."

Lymon watched as the towel was neatly tied into a bundle before it and his black tactical case vanished through the door.

"We could work something out." Sid cocked his head, indicating the gun-toting guards. "You don't need them. Why don't we just mosey over to the bar, crack a couple of those fancy bottles, and figure out what it would take to bring this to a satisfactory conclusion?"

"Why would I do that?" Hank walked a slow circle of the room, glancing at the ornate fixtures with mild interest. "Seems to me I've got you. Better, I've got every other card in your deck, including Bridges, Marks, and Anaya. I've even got an unseen hole card, Sid. I happen to know that nobody back at the barn knows where you are, or better yet, what you're working on."

Sid made a buzzer noise with his tongue, adding, "Wrong! No points for Hank this round. Sean O'Grady at the LAFO knows. It's all over the country. One lead after another piped from field office to field office."

"Nice bluff." Hank smiled. "We've had feelers out. No one's certain yet that we really kidnapped Christal. They'd just like to talk to us. We've been considering damage-control options. What if it turns out that sweet Christal went willingly?"

"Yeah, right," Lymon interjected. "You should have seen O'Grady's face when we told him you'd offered five grand just to see her."

"What makes you think she didn't take it?" Hank's mocking tone antagonized Lymon's sense of impotent rage.

Sid propped his hands on his hips. "I know Chris. Whatever you've done with her, she's not going to play ball."

Lymon saw the faintest hesitation in the guy's eyes. Yeah, Sid hit a nerve.

Hank turned, walking to stare out at the ocean through the large windows. "You people being here makes it a little more difficult. That's all. Not only that, Sid, you're on your own. Nobody in the Bureau is talking about Sheela Marks as bait—and you know they would. It's an agency—as hungry for juicy gossip as any other bunch of half-frustrated people." He laughed. "Hell, Marks' own business manager doesn't know what's coming off or why."

"And that's another screwup," Sid continued. "This is *Sheela Marks* we're talking about. Not just some grunt off the street. She's wise to you, and you can bet that people are going to be listening to her when she gets off this floating den of perversion."

Hank frowned. "We're going to have to give that some thought. If we let you all go, can we count on you to take it to the press? Do that, and by the end of the week, every person in the civilized world is going to know our name. When the swarms of reporters come clambering aboard, we can demonstrate our gene therapies, our enhancements, and successes in IVF. We couldn't *pay* for that kind of publicity."

"You'll be shut down within days. Your vessel confiscated, and each of you slapped with charges like you've never even imagined," Lymon added.

Hank whirled, a gleam in his eyes. "Oh, I don't think so."

"Why's that?" Sid asked.

"This is a Yemeni-flagged vessel in international waters. We are operating in compliance with Yemeni law. The official government of Yemen, if you'll recall, is an ally in the war against terrorism. At least the part that's not Houthi is. They're strategically located, providing us with bases of operation in the Red Sea, the Persian Gulf, and the Horn of Africa. Their government hands over suspected Islamic fundamentalists with terrorist ties in return for our support in the civil war. With all that at stake, do you really think Washington is going to compromise that relationship over a few strands of celebrity DNA?"

"You might be surprised," Sid said dryly.

"So might you." Hank cocked his head. "One of the things you're unaware of is how many Washington bigwigs the Sheik has treated aboard the *ZoeGen* and at the facility in Yemen. I was actually stunned when I read the list."

Lymon had been watching him, reading his body language. Damn it, either the guy was one hell of a poker player, or he really believed he held all the cards. He wasn't just bullshitting; he was bragging. And that, more than anything else, deepened the chill along Lymon's spine.

"Sheela Marks has a pretty loud voice herself," Lymon said. "And so, too, do Talia Roberts, Manny, and the rest of the celebrities whose DNA you've stolen. I think they can make it pretty hot for you."

Hank shrugged. "The average American thinks they're spoiled, rich, shallow, and for the most part, as moral as dock rats. You ever read the bios? Who's going to garner more sympathy? Ben Affleck, or a twelve-year-old little girl whose life Genesis Athena just saved through one of our miracle therapies?"

"The key is still Christal," Sid said doggedly. "That's kidnapping, and we'll get you for that."

Hank chuckled. "What makes you so sure about Christal? How do you know we haven't made her an offer she can't refuse? If we could pay five grand just to talk to her, what would we be willing to offer in return for her cooperation?" He stepped close, looking into Sid's eyes. "And we don't need Christal, Sid. What about you? For a million in cold hard cash, would you be willing to sign a statement that Christal told you she was here of her own free will?"

"Fuck you." Sid crossed his arms.

"Please, old friend, hands where we can see them. That's it." Hank leaned close. "Two million?"

Sid hesitated, the first uncertainty reflected in his expression. "You're shitting!"

"First thing every morning after a spicy meal," Hank replied. "But I'm not kidding about our ability to reward the people who work for us. Only one thing, Sid—you're going to have to prove you're worth it."

The door opened, and an attractive woman stuck her head in. She looked Lymon and Sid over with curious gray eyes, her long red hair falling around her shoulders. "Hank? We're set. The passengers are all in the dining room. The hallway is cleared."

"Thanks, April." Hank gestured at Lymon and Sid. "All right, you two, while you think over our offer, let's go."

"Where?" Sid asked, propping his feet as if to root himself in the rich carpet.

"Someplace safe," Hank answered. "Where you won't be upsetting our other passengers."

The Arab guards lifted their heavy black weapons. Lymon had seen that look before; it didn't bode well. Reluctantly, he waved Sid forward and started for the door.

CHAPTER 28

Visions spun and rolled behind Sheela's eyes. Her dreams seemed chaotic—pastiches of scenes acted, roles played, and people she'd known. She saw her father's face, smiling, worried... dead. Rex, beaming as he took her hand for the first time and said, "Sheela Marks, I think I can be of great service to you." Bernard, arms waving as he cried, "My god! That's masterful! Cut! Cut!" The weight of the Oscar—so cold and heavy in her hand—as thunderous ovation rolled up from the Kodak Theatre floor.

It all gave way to an image of Lymon: tall, muscular, his craggy face lit by a smile. He was reaching for her, his hand outstretched as he straddled his silver BMW. All she needed was to take his hand, step up on the passenger peg, and he'd wheel her away to forever: just the two of them and the magical motorcycle that sped her toward nirvana.

Awareness came from her physical body. Her attempt to swallow ended in disaster. Her tongue caught on the back of her mouth, almost choking her. She started, coughed, and blinked her dry eyes open.

The light was bleary, white, and streaked. She tried to swallow again and failed.

"Easy," a gentle female voice told her. "Let me help you."

A hand slipped behind her head, easing her forward. "Here's water. Just take a sip."

Sheela felt a glass touch her lips, and cool liquid washed around her tongue. When she swallowed, the water rolled through her chest and stomach like a wave.

Blinking again, the room slowly came into focus. And what a room! Marble columns, gold filigree in polished dark wood, thick Persian carpets, and what looked like a diamond-encrusted chandelier overhead. She lay on a velvet-upholstered chaise lounge, the woodwork polished and engraved. Bright white light came from large windows behind her.

She tried to place the white-clad nurse. "You are...?" Her voice cracked.

"Asza. You're aboard the *ZoeGen,* Ms. Marks."

Sheela groaned as she forced herself to sit up, arms bracing her on the cushions. She was half reclined on a couch of some sort. "Why am I here?"

A sibilant voice came from behind her left shoulder. "Because you paid us to impregnate you with a Sheela Marks embryo."

The nurse stepped back, and Sheela turned, seeing a dark and handsome man in an expensive silk suit. He had neatly combed black hair that gleamed, half silhouetted by sunlight shining through the windows. He looked Arab from his complexion, with a fine-boned face, intelligent eyes, and a smile that flashed perfect white teeth. He was standing before a golden espresso machine that sat atop an intricately carved wooden stand.

He spoke softly, barely audible over the hiss of the machine. "Imagine our surprise when we discovered that Jennifer Weaver's and Sheela Marks' DNA matched exactly. Fortunately, we discovered the situation before serious consequences could occur. So, no harm has been done."

Sheela reached up, rubbing her face. Her skin had the feel of dry latex.

He stepped forward, reaching out a hand. "I am Sheik Amud Abdulla, founder and president of Genesis Athena. Welcome aboard the *ZoeGen,* Ms. Marks. If I had known you were coming, I would have made a special effort and have greeted you as you came aboard. I have admired your work for years."

"Thank you." It was coming back now. The *ZoeGen*...Genesis Athena...a party of people bearing Christal away in the dead of night. "Why are you doing this?"

"I am building this century's quintessential service and health industry. Science has always laid the foundations for every great empire. You need only think of Alexander's iron swords, or Roman architecture and engineering, the English colonial factory system, or the modern American military-industrial complex. Personally, I would have preferred to develop the space industry. It would have been a much more natural extrapolation from my family's expertise in shipping across oceans to the transportation of goods across the solar system. Marshaling the capital, however, was not only prohibitive, but others like Musk and Bezos are so far ahead of us."

"Let me get this straight. You steal DNA because you can't go to space?"

"Each is part of mankind's future," the Sheik told her amiably as he stepped back and worked the levers on the coffee machine. Steam hissed. "Our world is becoming increasingly competitive. In the past, humans have focused on making ever more intricate, improved, and sophisticated tools. I offer the next step: that of producing ever better humans to use them."

"And for that, you needed *my* DNA?"

"To be sure, Ms. Marks. You are a most beautiful and intelligent woman. The same traits which make you so attractive add value to your DNA." As the machine sputtered, he raised a slim index finger to his chin, as though in deep thought. "What is celebrity?"

"It's a pain in the ass."

He might not have heard her snide remark. "It is envy, and what people envy, they wish to emulate. Through you, they live vicariously, be it by means of your screen presence or—with the help of Genesis Athena—your very genes."

"That's sick."

"I make no judgments. I simply provide a product in return for a fee. Our latest survey indicates that eight percent of the American people will pay to have a baby derived from their favorite celebrity's DNA. Eight percent! And that is without advertising, without incentives of any sort. Most, alas, are from lower-income, lower-educational demographics, but taken in total, they represent a substantial market. And that is just America. China, India, Indonesia, and Thailand, where cloning isn't viewed with as much suspicion, are worth billions more to us in the long run."

"Then why start with Americans?"

"In the modern world, Ms. Marks, marketing is everything, as you and your publicist well know."

"And the website? The questionnaire?"

"It allows us to rank-order potential clients. We can immediately discard the frivolous and closed-minded while concentrating on persons with both the predisposition and ability to afford our services."

"The way you talk of cloning it's another form of slavery."

He paced to one of the windows and stared out. "We are helping people to have children—nothing more, nothing less. The only difference between natural reproduction and our IVF service is the genotype of the child. It is still a life, Ms. Marks. As prized—or despised—by its parents as any other."

"That's the entire point!"

He turned, silhouetted by the glow. "Is there a difference between a life based on your DNA versus a child conceived of any other two people's? More than eight *billion* human beings exist on this planet; until recently, each of them was created by the chance mixture of parental DNA. You were created that way. Are you going to try and tell me that DNA that was good enough for you isn't good enough for someone else?"

"It's *my* DNA!"

"You had no part in its design, composition, or character. Even American law following the wake of the Myriad Genetics ruling declares it a 'natural' product. You received it from your biological parents, who in return, received theirs from their parents, and so on. If DNA is anyone's, it is God's."

"I don't see it the way you do."

"Ah, you would have me believe that your soul acted to choose your DNA? Perhaps pointed in the darkness of your mother's womb, saying, 'There! I want that sperm, and only that sperm, with those discrete genes to fertilize this egg and this egg alone!'"

"Don't be preposterous."

"Who," he asked mildly, "is being preposterous? You developed from a random association of deoxyribonucleic acids that programmed the synthesis of proteins into a specific pattern of organic compounds. You are the building, not the blueprint. And since you, yourself, didn't draw the blueprint, what do you care if we initiate the construction of additional buildings?"

"I'm going to tear you apart over this."

He chuckled, stepping back to watch as Sheela swung her feet unsteadily to the floor. Asza glanced at the Sheik, who made a small gesture with his fingers. The nurse bowed, walking on noiseless white shoes to let herself out through an ornate door. Sheela caught a glimpse of a suited guard outside. An automatic weapon hung ominously from a strap over his shoulder.

An armed guard? What was he afraid of? *Lymon!*

"Ms. Marks," the Sheik said as he filled a small cup with steaming coffee, "I am not an unreasonable man. I understand and feel for your confusion. As we speak, the world is unprepared for the reality of Genesis Athena."

"Got that right." She placed a hand to her stomach. That empty nauseous feeling had to be hunger. How long had it been since she'd eaten? She considered trying to stand and gave it up; her head was still woozy.

"Eventually, perhaps, there will be some consensus in international law about the disposition of an individual's DNA. Most governments, however, have been reluctant to venture into such murky and obscure waters."

"Why?"

He turned back to the machine, supple fingers plying the levers. "Politicians, for the most part, are not particularly bright or creative people. Look at the American abortion ban. Or the political idiocy over COVID vaccines. By nature, politicians look for the lowest common denominator that will get them elected. They do not take kindly to tackling intellectual challenges that will redefine the human condition. Thinking, especially about philosophical matters, causes them a great deal of distress. For the moment, they believe it is easier—and benefits society—to keep their hands off DNA. Think of it as the carrot offered to biotech firms for their investment in manipulating the human genome and discovering a host of other medical applications.

"And then there are the rising rates of infertility. Ever-lowering sperm counts are caused by phthalates and estrogenizing molecules. Male infertility is of growing concern, and birthrates are falling all across the industrialized world. The US, Europe, Japan, China, Russia, and others cannot replace their populations. Genesis Athena's therapies will soon be licensed worldwide."

"There's still time to change it." She smiled grimly.

"Who knows, I might just be the woman to push it through."

He shook his head as he filled a second cup of coffee. "I think not, Ms. Marks. The cat is out of the sack, and it would be way too much trouble to chase it down again." He looked up. "Cream or sugar?"

She felt a subtle vibration and barely sensed movement. The Sheik, too, seemed to hesitate, a faint frown marring his forehead. Then he dismissed it and lifted an eyebrow. "This is my own special blend, Ms. Marks. You must be famished by now."

"Black, please." Sheela gave in. The aroma of the coffee might have been the most wonderful thing she'd ever smelled. Her stomach growled.

As he handed her one of the delicate blue-and-white cups, he added, "I am also a realist. I understand that the value placed on your DNA is the result of your hard work, risk, and perseverance. In essence, but for your energy and talent, it would only be so many nucleic acids strung between pen-tase sugars. A mere one of eight billion, if you will."

"What a delightful way to think of it."

"But valid, nonetheless."

"And?"

"And I am willing to offer you a royalty on all revenues we make off your genotype. If you involve yourself in the sales and marketing, we would be happy to offer you a higher percentage, one negotiated based on your participation. But for now, if we assume all obligation for marketing and publicity, we will send you a statement biannually for three percent of our net."

Shit! He was serious. *He wanted her to help sell her clones!*

"I'm sorry it can't be more, but one never knows. You might take some action which damages the value before we recoup our investment in you."

"Such as?"

His shoulder lifted slightly. "We know the genetic and degenerative diseases you are predisposed to and can compensate for them, but what if you ruin our investment through a willful act?"

"How could I do that?" She tried to keep the anticipation out of her voice.

"Suicide."

An image of her father's face flashed in her mind as she said flatly, "Not a chance."

"Questionable religious or political associations could damage your value." His lips quirked. "Say, a newfound affiliation with right-wing white supremacists or offensive cults."

"Neo-Nazis? I think that's a bit unlikely. As to the mindless cults, I'll stay away from both Democrats *and* Republicans."

"You might become involved in criminal activity such as drug dealing, involvement in homicide, or sexual aberrations with children or livestock."

Livestock?

She shook her head and made a face. "Maybe you've guessed, but I didn't come here looking for money."

"Indeed?" He gave her a grim smile. "Then what?"

Before she could answer, he said, "Ah, but of course, justice! The great grail to which we all aspire in the end." His thin lips curled. "And just how, Ms. Marks, did you intend on obtaining your justice? Perhaps through a legal suit, since your attorney was the only party privy to your arrival?"

"How did you know that?"

He shrugged off her question. "We operate in international waters. You would have to file suit against us in a Yemeni court. I am a personal friend and supporter of Rashad al-Alimi who leads the current government. Our law is Islamic. I don't think you would appreciate or approve of the final judgment."

"Your people stole my DNA in the United States."

"For which I deeply apologize and offer a financial restitution." He shrugged. "What is your embarrassment worth, Ms. Marks? Perhaps I could make a fifty percent investment in your next film?"

"Look, I want my stolen DNA destroyed. I want your guarantee that you won't use it to make little Sheela babies. You do that, and I'll collect my people—including Christal Anaya—and be out of here on the next boat. After that, you and I will have no further association. Deal?"

He studied her through half-lidded eyes. "Ms. Marks, you are a formidable woman, but you are not in any position to be making demands. Genesis Athena has fulfilled its obligations to you. I have given you my offer. I think it is a very generous one." His smile sharpened. "Do you wish to accept?"

"No, actually, I think we'll do this the hard way. In the courts." She tried to stand, swayed, and sat down again, clutching at her empty coffee cup.

"You will need time to recover from the anesthetic, Ms. Marks," the Sheik observed dryly. "Perhaps we will talk again when you're feeling a little better." He raised his voice, calling, *"Achmed!"*

The door opened to reveal the armed guard. A quick mix of Arabic passed between them, and Asza appeared with a wheelchair. She smiled as she locked the wheels in front of Sheela, asking, "Are you ready, Ms. Marks?"

"For what?"

"I'm here to take you back to your quarters. You'll feel a great deal better after you've eaten and slept."

She helped Sheela move into the wheelchair. "Thanks for the coffee," Sheela called over her shoulder. "But we're not through yet."

His waspish smile mocked her. "No. But we will be...and very soon, Ms. Marks."

The door cut off any reply.

CHAPTER 29

By placing heel to toe, Lymon could make eight steps in one direction and five in the other. The cramped steel cubicle had been painted in thick layers of white, and a single recessed bulb glowed from behind a wire mesh screwed to the ceiling. The heavy waterproof hatch that opened to the corridor had been firmly dogged. Whoever the thoughtful party had been who had remodeled it, he'd forgotten to leave a handle on the inside.

The room was naked of fixtures or furniture. Sid squatted in one corner, a tired look on his face. His hands were limply propped on his knees, wrists protruding from his rumpled suit coat. Standing above him, Lymon could see Sid's scalp beginning to gleam through sparse dark hair on the top of his head. God, Sid was too fucking young to be going bald.

"Sorry I got you into this," Lymon told him hollowly.

"Wasn't your fault, boss. I sent Christal to you, if

you'll recall." He smiled sheepishly. "Funny thing about Christal. Shit just happens around her. But for her, we'd have never found the lynchpin that tied my geneticists to your tampon theft. It's like—hell, I don't know—she's some sort of lightning magnet, you know?"

"Believe me, I've been figuring that out." Lymon paced anxiously back to the door, shoving on it with all his might. That did him about as much good as dining on dinosaurs.

Lymon felt a faint vibration through the hull and a subtle shift in his balance. They were moving. Headed where? Farther out to sea where the bodies wouldn't be washing into the shipping lanes the way Nancy Hartlee's had?

Sid said, "You know, I believe that story about her grandma being a witch. It has to be some deep-seated occult thing. Nobody else could draw this much shit down." He frowned. "Assuming Christal's here."

"Her kidnappers are here, which means they probably brought her here." Lymon smacked the thick hatch with the meaty bottom of his fist. "No, actually, I hope she's someplace else. This is starting to look a little grim. You felt this thing start to move?"

"Yep. And I don't think they're headed to the Navy pier in Manhattan, either." A pause. "How do you think they got onto us so fast? Neal Gray?"

"Maybe. Hell, it could have been Hank. He might have seen us come aboard." Lymon shook his head. "They were ahead of us from step one. As soon as they had us separated, they took Sheela. Then, when they had the other clients safely out of the way, they swept us up like bugs on a waxed hardwood floor."

Sid smacked his lips, the frown deepening on his forehead. "So, what do you think they're going to do with us?"

"What can they? Charge us with bringing guns aboard?" Lymon slapped his arms to his side, lying: "Nah, my guess is that they're putting pressure on Sheela, and when it's all finished, and she agrees to whatever they want, we'll be bundled aboard that launch and sent back to shore."

Sid gave him a flat look.

"What else can they do?" Lymon insisted, trying to believe it himself. "You're an FBI agent. People are going to be missing you. There's a kidnapping involved. *Sheela* is here. They've got to cut some kind of deal with her. Whatever it is, we'll be part of it."

"Uh-huh." Sid stared at his hands, expression tight. "You know, I never did right by Claire."

"What the hell brought that in out of the blue?"

"I should have treated her better." He looked away. "She always hated DC."

"So, when you get out of here, move someplace else."

"I will." But he said it flatly, then looked up. "Lymon, let's be honest, shall we? We know an awful lot about them. Who their people are, what they're doing."

"You're a federal agent. They won't mess with you."

"Joe Hanson, one of the guys at the WMFO, was taken out when I first got assigned there. Held hostage for a couple of days. The bad guys liquored him up and drove him off a cliff. Being an agent isn't always sacrosanct."

"Sheela will work it out." Lymon rubbed the back of

his neck. "One way or another, it's going to mean a chunk out of her hide, but she'll do it."

"And then?"

"You and I will spend the rest of our lives worshipping at her feet. I don't know what they'll ask of her, but you can bet it won't be easy."

Sid was watching Him. "She'd do that? Sell her soul to save us?"

Lymon sighed, nodded reluctantly, and sank down on the cold steel floor. "You don't know her like I do. It's the price she's always had to pay to do what had to be done. She gives up little pieces of her soul for other people. Most of them, like Rex, are sophisticated cannibals who devour her bit by tiny bit. It's a wonder she's not a hollow shell these days."

"Yeah, well, I hope for both our sakes that you're right."

For long moments Lymon fixed his gaze on the endless white of their tiny cell. "It's all backward. I'm supposed to be saving her. It's my job."

Silence.

Sid softly asked, "You think Christal's all right?"

"Yeah." But he didn't mean it. "How'd Hank Abrams end up being such a shit?"

"Bad genes."

They stared at each other for a moment.

"The guy's always been an asshole." Sid rubbed a hand over his face. "You just cut an asshole a little more slack if he happens to be on your team."

"What turned him to the Dark side?"

"Money, ambition, the chance to screw Christal—" Sid went white. "Shit, you don't think..."

Lymon pursed his lips. "Maybe. It's a crummy

world. Assuming we're all dropped someplace with our hearts still beating and allowed to go home, we're going to have to treat those ladies with a great deal of compassion and care."

"You think that's the price of our freedom?"

Lymon studied the calluses on his hands. "If that's what it takes to buy our freedom, Sheela will go through with it. But what about later? What do you say when you're looking her in the eyes? 'Thank you' sounds a little trite. Where do you find the words to tell her the things in your soul?"

"Beats me."

They stared at the walls in silence then, waiting, for...what?

"Think they'll ever feed us?"

"Hank didn't strike me as a compassionate and caring kind of guy."

Lymon took a deep breath and closed his eyes. Put one finger on the pulse in his wrist. He was fully aware of each beat of his heart. How much longer was he going to be able to enjoy that sensation?

Truth was, Sid had a high probability of being right. It would be just as easy to march them to the railing in the middle of the night, pop a cap into each of their skulls, and let them drop over the side. As to Sheela, she could disappear into some mansion in the Yemeni backcountry, and no one would be the wiser. Christal? For all he knew, she'd already fallen prey to something terrible.

He was so lost in his thoughts he didn't hear the greased dogs on the hatch slide back. It was Sid's elbow that brought him to his feet. He started and gaped.

Christal Anaya stood in the open hatch, a heavy bag hanging from one hand. She was decked out in a too-tight white nurse's uniform. Grinning, she said, "Hi, boss. Hi, Sid. So, tell me, did I miss much?"

CHAPTER 30

As Christal swung the heavy bag across the room to Lymon, she said, "I found that on a table in the security center. All those guns and a flash-bang! I'd never have guessed they were yours except for the billfolds, and I'd know Sid's lock-picks anywhere."

"How the hell did you find us?" Sid cried, stepping forward to throw his arms around her.

"I was having the most fascinating talk with a guy named Vince up in the security center. Did you know that they've got the most incredible system of cameras and microphones on this boat? You can hear a mouse fart three decks away."

She watched Lymon work the slide to check the round in the chamber and then shove the HK .40 Compact into its underarm holster.

Sid—grinning from ear to ear—let her loose, asking, "Are you all right?" as he took his turn at the bag. His smile split his face as he stuffed his precious lockpicks and his billfold into pockets. Last came a set of keys, a small Maglite, and a Spyderco folder.

"Fine, but we'd better be rolling. We're two decks down from the security center. It's not far, but it's still dicey. I could have left you here, safe, but I took a chance on springing you when I did. It's a gamble either way."

"Where's the other pistol?" Sid asked as he shoved his billfold into his back pocket.

"I've got it. Let's beat feet." She turned, starting down the corridor and pulling the HK Compact from her right hip pocket. "This isn't a sure thing by any means. A whole lot of shit could still come down."

"Where are Hank and his goons?" Lymon asked from behind her.

"Right now they're in a strategy session with the Sheik. Sheela was up in his stateroom, or whatever the hell you call it. It's like a castle atop the A Deck behind the stack. Pretty ritzy chunk of real estate, I'd guess. It's also the only place on this hulk that isn't wired."

"You saw Sheela?"

"Yeah." Christal shot a hard look over her shoulder. "She looks a little wobbly. Just a guess, mind you, but I think they're keeping her disoriented, maybe as a means of softening her up, or maybe it's just for security reasons."

"How long have you been here?" Sid asked.

"Seems like forever. I don't know. Last thing I remember was going home with groceries in LA, seeing Hank behind me on the steps, and *bam!* waking up here."

"They just let you wander around?" Lymon asked as he stuffed things from the bag into his pockets.

She gave him the look she reserved for idiots, and added, "Boss, if they catch any of us, they'll shoot first and ask questions later."

Lymon was eyeing the cameras they hurried past.

"It's all right," Christal told him. "As long as our luck holds, no one's at the monitors. But we sure as hell don't want to loaf."

"What about your friend, Vince?" Lymon shot a fast glance back the way they'd come. "I've had conversations with him before. He didn't seem like the fun and forgiving kind."

"He's having a very close-up-and-personal encounter with a roll of duct tape." She led them up a stairway. "Boss, there's one thing you need to know."

"Lay it on me."

"No matter what happens, no matter to whom it happens, we've got to keep them distracted for another hour and fifteen minutes. Do you understand?"

God, hold it together up there, Brian! She prayed to herself. She'd bet everything on the geneticist.

"What happens in an hour and fifteen minutes?" Sid asked.

"If we last that long, life is going to get really interesting for Genesis Athena."

Christal trotted up a second stairway, took a hard right, and stopped at a thick steel door marked SECURITY. "Pray for a miracle," she muttered, raising the pistol with one hand and pushing with the other. A thick fold of paper fell away as the door swung inward.

"Whew!" she exhaled as she stepped through, covering the room with the powerful HK pistol. "Nobody here but us mice. Get the door, Sid. Make sure it's closed." She stepped over to where she could see Vince behind one table. He still looked like a silver pupa. Behind the other, Gregor McEwan stared up from the duct tape like a bug-eyed worm.

"What's this?" Lymon had the fold of paper in his hand.

"To keep the door from locking behind me."

Sid and Lymon were staring, wide-eyed, at the entire wall covered with monitors showing various views of the corridors, decks, and hatches. Here and there, images flipped from one scene to another as someone walked into the camera's eye.

"Sid," she called, "keep an eye on the monitors. The security hatch is the one in the upper left. Holler if anyone tries to get in. Vince wouldn't tell me whether anybody can open the door. It's got a lock plate on the outside, and who knows how many people have the code."

"Neal Gray for sure," Lymon said, striding up to look down at the bound and gagged men. "Friends of yours?"

"That's Vince," she said, pointing. "He's the one who looks like a silver mummy. Sort of handsome actually, but you can only see his eyes. He's got a short beard, but I'm betting three-to-one odds that most of it goes when someone finally pulls the tape off."

Vince's eyes rolled in an unsettled manner, and he made mumbling sounds through the little hole where his nostrils weren't covered.

"And this is?" Lymon indicated the second man.

"Meet Dr. Gregor McEwan. Late head of the Genesis Athena genetics program."

"McEwan?" Sid asked, looking up from the huge bank of monitors. "Scottish? Midthirties, light-brown hair, brown eyes, kind of a round face?"

"That's him."

"Yahoo! He's one of my kidnap victims!"

"Not anymore. He changed sides." Christal tapped her pistol meaningfully as Gregor watched.

Lymon studied the security system, looking from the monitors down to the knobs. "Where's Sheela?"

"One of the nurses was wheeling her down to her room last I saw." Christal glanced up. "Time was short. You were closer and didn't have an armed guard following behind you."

Lymon tapped something into the computer and muttered, "Whoops" when the screens went dark. He hit *Esc* and they came on again.

"Don't fart around, boss," Sid growled at him.

Lymon turned to Christal. "How'd you get here?"

She sighed, fingering the polymer grip of the HK pistol. "I was down in the high-security area when I asked a friend if they'd cloned any Terminators, you know, from the movie? He said no, but I remembered Linda Hamilton sticking a needle full of drain cleaner into a bad guy's neck. So the next time Gregor came in, we stuck a needle into his side, and he walked us out. I was playing his girlfriend in the elevator when I saw him staring hopefully at the security camera."

"So, you came here first?" Lymon asked.

"We couldn't do anything until we controlled the security center. Gregor very persuasively talked Vince into opening the door." She gestured at the monitors. "This is the high ground, boss."

"You said you had a partner?" Sid asked.

"Yeah, Brian Everly, he's—"

"The Australian geneticist?" Sid asked, turning. "The guy who disappeared from Australia?"

"Yeah, that's him." She lifted an eyebrow. "Nice guy, too. For the time being, he's cooling his heels and staying out of trouble in—"

"Whoa!" Lymon interrupted, pointing. "Bad guy alert! We've got movement! That's Neal Gray, and there's our friend Hank Abrams stepping into the elevator along with the redhead."

Christal followed his finger to a monitor displaying a group of people as the elevator doors slid shut. "The woman is April Hayes. She's my Copperhead from LA. They're kind of the Genesis Athena brain trust for covert operations."

They watched the monitor as the cage descended. Christal felt her gut tightening as she studied the faces. At that moment, a white dot appeared at the corner of the screen, and Sid cried, "Got it!" He was fiddling with a mouse on a pad beside the control board.

A half second later, the image shifted to the big central screen, and the audio kicked on.

Neal Gray was saying, "*...depends on Marks. In the meantime, April, I want you to run down to H Deck and find out where McEwan is. It's not like that asshole to miss a meeting.*"

"*On my way,*" April said as the elevator door slid open. Text at the bottom of the screen told them the cage was on C Deck.

Abrams and Gray stepped out, and Christal saw them emerge onto one of the smaller monitors.

"Which one do we follow?" Sid asked.

"Go for Hank and Neal," Lymon replied.

"I'll keep an eye on Copperhead." Christal watched as the monitors shifted. Hayes rode the lift down to H Deck and stepped out. The image on the monitor constantly shifted, as one by one, the complicated computer program sorted from camera to camera as it followed her the short distance, and around the corner. Christal watched Copperhead approach the security entrance and ring her way through.

Hayes stopped short in the box, staring through the glass at Max. Her mouth worked, and Max spoke in reply, hunching his shoulders as if in confusion.

Hayes frowned, asking something further.

Max bent down, fingers running over the control board as he watched the various monitors to either side. After a moment, he shook his head.

Christal could almost read Copperhead's lips as she said, "Then where is he?"

"Trouble, people." Christal straightened as Max lifted a phone to his ear and punched a number. The phone by Lymon's left hand bleated.

"That's Max," Christal said. "He's calling, trying to find out where Gregor is."

"So?"

"So, answer it! Pretend you're Vince and say that Gregor went to his quarters to boff his sweetie."

"What makes you think I can sound like Vince?" But Lymon was already lifting the receiver, saying in a bored voice, "Security center, what do you need, Max?"

Lymon listened as Christal watched the face on the monitor. Max looked slightly puzzled but was talking.

"He's in his quarters doing his girl." Lymon spoke with a slight wryness to his voice. After a pause, he said, "Got me." And hung up.

Max was staring thoughtfully at the phone; then he looked straight into the monitor, as if trying to see behind the camera. Christal would have given anything to hear what he said to Copperhead, who in turn stared up at the camera with thoughtful eyes.

"Can we switch this?" Christal asked.

"Wait." Sid was watching Abrams and Gray as they entered what appeared to be a lounge. A big conference table was surrounded by chairs. Several men, Arab from their looks, sat drinking sodas, smoking cigarettes, and talking. They looked up when Hank and Neal entered.

"Heads up," Neal said as he stopped at the table. *"We've got a situation developing."*

"There's got to be a way to listen to both monitors at once!" Christal growled as she stared impotently at the keyboard controls. Glancing up, she watched as Copperhead stepped out of the controlled entrance and fiddled with a lock plate. Before the camera went dead, Christal got a glimpse into the control room where Max was sitting. The screen obligingly switched to an Arab woman scrubbing a section of I Deck.

"Damn!" Christal knotted a fist, glaring at the monitor.

"We don't know yet what our options are going to be. Marks may or may not cooperate. If she doesn't, the police are going to find her drugged to incoherence in her hotel room in Jamaica. We'll leave enough cocaine scattered around to keep her and her lawyers entertained for a decade."

"What about her security?" one of the Arab guys asked.

"We haven't decided that yet. If they can't be bought off, it may be more economical for the LAPD to find a stash of

drugs in Bridges' house. They'll tie it to Marks' Jamaican binge. We can accomplish that for as little as ten thousand paid to the right people."

"Sons of bitches!" Sid bellowed.

"I need to get Copperhead back," Christal said, frantically reaching down to tap the *Backspace* button on the control keyboard. Nothing happened. She could hear Vince snickering against the tape from behind the table. For an instant, she considered walking back and booting him real hard in the ribs, but gave it up as the sound of a pager came through the speakers. On-screen, Neal Gray reached for his small belt radio.

Copperhead's voice barked from one of the control room speakers, saying, *"Neal? Cracked Castle. Go now."*

They watched Neal switch channels on his belt radio before lifting it to his ear. After saying, *"Yeah," "Uh-huh,"* and *"Keep me informed,"* Gray turned, saying to Abrams, *"April and Max can't find Anaya. They think she's out with Everly and McEwan. She and Max are reviewing the tapes right now."*

Hank frowned, lifting his own belt radio and pressing a button. Hank's voice asked, "Vince?" from the speaker.

Lymon gave Sid a knowing glance and picked up the microphone, saying, "Security, Vince."

Christal heard Hank ask, *"Do you have the location of —"* Hank frowned on-screen, glancing up as if to stare at them through the monitor. *"Who is this?"*

"Vince," Lymon said in a bored voice. "Just like every day at this time. What do you need, Hank?"

Christal was staring into Hank's eyes as his frown deepened and he lowered the phone. She could see his mind racing, trying to put the pieces together. "He's not buying it."

"Oh, shit," Lymon muttered as he set the mic back on the desk. Abrams had leaned close to Gray's ear, whispering. Then they both turned to stare up at the camera.

CHAPTER 31

On the main monitor in the security center, Abrams and Gray continued their whispered conversation on the main monitor. Then they started around the room, whispering into the ears of each of the other security personnel. As they did, one by one, black pairs of eyes turned toward the camera. The expressions were anything but friendly.

Christal would have given anything to know what they were plotting as she tried to figure out the controls to the security system.

"Looks like the bad guys have settled on a plan," Lymon announced. "Whatever they're cooking up, it's not going to be good."

"Nope," Sid muttered. "Hope this room doesn't turn into the Alamo."

Christal kept an eye on Lymon as he stepped to the cabinets at the back of the room. He pulled the doors open one by one, finding electrical equipment, assorted cables, and conduit in one. Life jackets in another, tools and what looked like spare parts in a third. Paper supplies in a fourth. Another held gas masks and protective gear. A fire extinguisher hung on a bracket beside the hatch.

"Christal?" Lymon asked. "When you arrived here, our guns and stuff were on one of the tables, right?"

"Affirmative. That one there." She pointed.

"But was there a big black plastic case?"

"Sorry, boss, it's already up on the bridge."

"Damn!" He slammed the last locker and glanced down at the duct-tape-swathed men.

Christal followed his gaze to see that Vince had wiggled slightly to one side. From the amount of tape wrapped around him, he wasn't getting free anytime soon. McEwan just stared with a glum resignation in his worried brown eyes. Most likely considering what the Sheik was going to do to him for letting Christal make her escape.

"If we're going to do something, we'd better be on it fast," Christal called. "Copperhead is on the move, and she's talking into her radio. It's not coming through here. Cracked Castle must be their code to change band lengths." She studied the complicated control board. "If we only knew how to use this."

"Evidently she's in contact with Gray," Sid replied, "because he's whispering into his as well."

"We're moving," Lymon decided. "We've got seconds to wreck this place and go."

"Negative," Christal said, jabbing her thumb over her shoulder. "We've got McEwan. He's a major player. Worth a bundle to us as a hostage."

"And they'll have Sheela if we don't get to her ASAP," Lymon shot back sharply.

"You go," Christal told him. From the desperation in

Lymon's eyes, there was going to be no stopping him. And more than anything, they needed to buy time.

She reached into one of the lockers he'd opened and lifted a pair of the belt radios. Pressing the button, she said, "Testing." One of the room speakers crackled and repeated it. She tossed him the belt radio. "I'll hold the fort here and try to break their communications frequency."

Sid stood, taking the other radio. "I'm with Lymon."

"No!" Lymon shot him a knowing smile. "Get the hell off this thing. Someone's got to get the facts to the authorities."

"Hurry!" Christal cried, watching the monitors. "They're headed this way. You've only got seconds."

Sid stepped to the hatch, undogged it, and leaped out into the hallway. Lymon was hot on his heels. When the heavy hatch swung shut, the lock clicked with finality. Christal watched as the security system followed their flight.

They were in the middle of C Deck. Sheela was aft on B Deck, past the security hatches. Here and there in the cameras, men were emerging from cabins and hurrying along the corridors. For the moment, Lymon and Sid seemed to have a straight shot aft, through the security hatch, and up the stairs.

So, what needed to be done? Christal studied the big hatch, her point of vulnerability. Shore it up? A thick wad of electrical cable had spilled out of one of the lockers Lymon had pulled open. This she dragged to the hatch, along with several lengths of metal conduit. She pulled out a drawer on one side and wedged the conduit behind the fire extinguisher bracket on the wall on the other. Then she used the electrical cable to lash the conduit across the hatch wheel so that it couldn't be turned from the outside. Finally, she took one of the chairs, cramming it under the wheel for additional bracing.

Only then did she slip into the command chair and stare up at the monitors. Lymon and Sid were running full bore down a passageway listed as C Left on the screen.

In the screen above them, two guys in suits—security from the lounge—were running the opposite way in B Left.

"I get it," Christal whispered as she studied the screens. Each level of screens matched the different decks. She was watching figures on the left side, no doubt for the port side of the ship.

She lifted the large microphone that rested to the side and keyed it. Anyone with a radio would overhear her. "Lymon? You there?"

She watched him lift his radio. *"Here!"*

"Bogies at twelve o'clock. B Deck."

He seemed to get it. *"Roger."*

In the right-hand monitor that covered C Deck, she could see Copperhead stepping out of the elevator before hurrying down the hallway and taking a right. Christal watched the woman come to a stop right outside the security center hatch.

"Knock, knock," Christal said softly as she picked up the HK Compact, rocked the slide back to visually check the chamber, and let it slip back over the reassuring gleam of brass.

April Hayes punched a short sequence into the lock plate, saw it gleam green, and tried to turn the wheel that would open the hatch.

Christal watched the wheel move a couple of degrees before it bound tight on the electrical cable. In the monitor, April was straining against it, face in a grimace. Then she stepped back to raise her belt radio.

"Oh, my," Christal said sympathetically. "We just don't look happy today, do we?"

She glanced at the clock. They had forty minutes left. Time enough for everything to go terribly wrong.

CHAPTER 32

Sheela ate like she'd been away from food for days. The nurse, Asza, fiddled with the room service cart that had been delivered to the suite. Just inside the door, Achmed stood at ease, his ominous black HK submachine gun hanging from its sling. His face remained expressionless, eyes flat.

As if I were some sort of threat!

Sheela shook the thought off and continued cutting sections of steak into cubes before wolfing them. She had no idea what the future was going to bring; the opportunity to eat couldn't be turned down. Supper consisted of creamed corn, beef steak, mashed potatoes, and lobster tail.

She could feel herself coming alert again as her blood sugars began to rise. The last of the lethargy created by the anesthetic was wearing off. Still, she had a feeling of fatigue, as if the stress were nibbling at her bones. An unfamiliar tenderness lay deep within her belly. Aftereffects of the hormone shot?

"Why are you involved in this?" she asked Asza.

"I serve my family," the woman told her evenly. "It is a great opportunity for me. Here I am valued, well paid, and I get to see so much of the world."

"Stealing other people's souls is valued work?"

Asza looked back quizzically. "I do not steal anyone's soul." She tapped her breast. "The soul is in here."

"What of the babies you plant in other women?"

"Allah will give them each a soul of their own." Asza lifted a spoon from one of the dishes on the cart. "Would you like some more corn?"

She indicated the guard. "What's his purpose? To shoot me if I try to leave?"

"He is here for your protection."

"Right."

She was considering testing the limits of her protection when her door opened and two men burst into the room. Sheela froze, fork halfway to her mouth.

"Get her up and get her out of here!" the first, a tall blond man in an immaculate suit, ordered.

"Just who do you think you are?" Sheela demanded as the second man—younger, brunette, with a handsome face—rounded the table, waved Asza aside, and grasped Sheela's elbow.

"Ms. Marks," he said, "I'm afraid we're going to have to cut supper short."

"But I—" She was jerked to her feet, almost fell as her chair toppled backward, and was shoved forward, reeling to catch her balance.

"Get her out of here, Hank!" the gray-clad man told the younger. "To the Sheik's. Fast!"

"On the way," Hank agreed. "Asza, keep an eye out behind us. Good luck, Neal."

Asza followed behind as the young man hurried Sheela toward the door.

"You," Neal told the guard, who was looking uncertainly back and forth. "Give me a hand."

The last thing Sheela saw as she was dragged through the door was Neal and her guard upending the dinner table, spilling plates and food all over the floor. As she stumbled down the hallway, a door opened, and Wyla Smith gaped, her mouth round with surprise.

"Call nine-one-one," Sheela called, only to have Hank twist her arm until she screamed. Whatever was happening, it wasn't going to be good.

CHAPTER 33

"L*ymon! You've got goons coming your way from both directions!*" Christal's voice came over the radio. "*Find a hole if you can.*"

"Roger." He glanced at Sid as they hurried down a Spartan hallway marred by sturdy-looking wooden doors. He gestured. "Try your side." And started rattling knobs on the left.

Sid grabbed knob after knob as they ran. "Here!" He found an open one on the left, leaping inside as Lymon, catching sight of the hatch opening ahead of them, pivoted on a foot and threw himself in behind Sid.

Sid clicked the door shut and leaned against it. They were both panting for breath as Lymon turned to survey their retreat. The first thing he noticed was that it looked like a small living room—the sort one might find in a mobile home. A TV in one corner was playing a daytime soap. On opposite ends of an overstuffed couch sat two women, staring wide-eyed and clearly startled by Lymon's sudden appearance. Each suckled an infant on an exposed breast.

Even as he gaped, both women pawed frantically to cover themselves, disrupting the babies, who bawled out in frustration.

"Sorry!" Lymon said, raising his hands—only to be brutally aware of the radio in one, and pistol in the other. "Security, ma'am," he made up, trying to grin sheepishly.

"Who are you?" the first young woman, a twenty-something brunette, managed. Her eyes were fixed on Lymon's pistol, as if she were staring at her own impending execution. She had the squalling baby tucked tightly against her stomach, where it kicked and punched from around the protection of her arms.

"I'm Rick, and he's Louie," Lymon lied between panted breaths. "Please, relax. This is just a training exercise."

"Where's the bogie?" Sid asked into his radio, eyes on the door.

"Still in the hall," Christal's voice returned. *"They're proceeding slowly, carefully. They've just spotted the second party and are moving toward them."*

"What model is that?" Lymon asked, indicating the brunette's infant.

She shot a quick glance at the blonde across from her, then said uneasily, "Elvis. They both are. We just delivered last week." She frowned. "You're sure you're security?"

"Yeah, Neal's got us on an exercise. Training, you know. Tactical evasion." He grinned, having almost caught his breath. "Hey, look, we apologize for just bursting in on you like this, but it's one of those 'make it up as you go along' things."

Sid was staring incredulously at the two women and their babies. "Elvis? As in Presley?"

Both women nodded, wariness barely abated.

"Yours?" Lymon asked as if just making conversation. "I mean, you both delivered in the normal way?"

Both women nodded in unison.

"Why Elvis?" Sid asked.

"He's the king," the brunette said as if that explained everything. "Look, don't you guys ever knock?" She was starting to recover. "I mean, damn! Dr. Morris said we'd have our privacy until we finished our postnatal physicals."

"Listen, we're really really sorry." Lymon gave Sid a meaningful glance as he raised his phone to ask, "Central, sit-rep, please."

"Bogie is at end of corridor. One moment. You're clear for the moment. Be aware of moving patrols."

"Roger." Lymon indicated the door. "Let's go, Louie."

Sid waved toward the women. "Good luck. Hope he can sing when he grows up."

Lymon cracked the door and glanced out to find the hallway empty. Sid closed the door behind them on the way out, then asked, "Rick and Louie?"

"Didn't you ever watch *Casablanca*?"

"I prefer car chases and explosions." Then, as they ran, "You believe that crap, that those kids were Elvis knockoffs?"

"The really scary thing is, yeah, I believe it."

Lymon trotted for the hatch, grabbed the wheel, and turned it. This was the moment of truth. They knew it was locked from the other direction. The dogs slid, and he stepped through, seeing an intersection of corridors along with a stairway leading up to B Deck. Evidently access wasn't restricted as you went aft. He glanced at the lock pad as the hatch clicked behind them. Going back wasn't going to be so easy.

"If our guesses are correct, we're right below—"

The radio crackled. *"Lymon! Bad news. They've got Sheela. She's one deck up. Better hurry."*

Lymon charged across the hallway, hammering his way up the staircase. He rounded the landing, heading up the last flight, and ran smack into one of the steel gratings. He could hear the ding as the elevator door clicked shut.

"Shit!" He gestured at the lock. "Get on it, Sid. Faster this time."

Sid fumbled out his lockpicks and bent to the task.

Lymon lifted the radio. "Where are they taking her? Can you tell?"

"Hang on, boss. I got troubles of my own."

CHAPTER 34

Christal watched four muscular men join up with Copperhead. The corridor outside the security center was getting way too crowded. As the latter glared up at the camera, one of the men punched in the security code; then all four massed their weight against the wheel.

With a sense of desperation, Christal took a deep breath and leveled her pistol on the hatch. "No matter what," she promised, "you're not coming through."

The wheel turned, straining the cable tighter around the conduit. She could see the wheel shivering as the cable stretched, resisted, and held. The hatch remained inviolate until the men finally released it and shook their heads.

Christal sighed with relief, letting the adrenaline seep out of her muscles.

April raised her radio, changed channels, and said through the speakers, "*I assume that is you in there, Ms. Anaya.*"

Christal lifted the radio. "Two things, April: One, I'll

shoot the first bastard to walk through that door—assuming, that is, that you can force it. Two, before you take me out, I'll put a bullet in Gregor McEwan's head."

Copperhead's stalwart gaze seemed to burn right through the lens. *"Let me talk to Gregor."*

"I think not. Bad form and all. You might have some other silly code like 'Cracked Castle.'"

"Then how do I know you've got him ?"

"Sometimes you just have to take things on faith." She smiled ironically. "Or the fact that you can't find him anywhere else in the ship."

"You know you can't win. Not in the end. Eventually you're going to run out of water, food, perhaps even oxygen."

"We'll deal with that when we get there."

She glanced at the line of monitors, watching as Lymon and Sid slid a steel grating aside to pile out onto the B Deck. Lymon turned and headed toward Sheela's quarters. Christal keyed her mic. "Lymon! Don't do it! She's not there."

Lymon slid to a halt, pausing uncertainly as he raised his radio. *"Where'd they take her?"*

"Deck A. The Sheik's."

In the hatch monitor, Copperhead was talking into her radio.

Christal felt the tension rising. "Lymon, April heard that. Beat feet, boss. Get the hell out of Dodge. Be aware that all communications are monitored from here on out."

"Ten-four." She watched as Lymon and Sid talked, then split, each running a different way down the corridor.

"So"—Copperhead's voice came through the

system—*"Bridges and Harness are loose? My, but you are a pain in the ass, Anaya."* April held the radio at an angle beside her jaw, a wry look on her face. *"Are you sure you wouldn't like to go to work for us? Anyone as talented and adventurous as you would make an incredible asset to the organization."*

Christal glanced up at the clock. Shit, the second hand seemed to crawl across the face. "How much?"

"Five hundred thousand a year, plus bonuses and royalties."

"Last I heard, it was two hundred grand."

"I think we misjudged your initial worth."

"Yeah, keep right on misjudging."

She watched as Lymon slid to a halt and pressed the button beside the elevator. Two men were approaching the B Deck security hatch from the forward corridor. Christal cued her mic. "Run, Lymon. No time."

He turned, beating down the hallway, feet flying. It was at that moment that Neal Gray and a second man stepped out of Sheela's door. The agent who followed dropped into position, the black sub gun centering on Lymon's chest.

"No!" Christal cried, starting out of the chair.

At precisely that moment the second team rounded the corner and charged into the corridor behind him. The shooter hesitated, afraid his burst would hit his companions.

"Give up, Lymon!" Christal said woodenly into her mic. "They've got you boxed, and you were just a couple of ounces away from being hamburger."

She could see the defeat reflected on his face as he let the pistol drop and raised his hands. Gray and the others closed on him. In a knot, they hustled him along to the elevator, waited for the door, and then Christal watched Lymon being lifted to the A Deck. The last she saw, he disappeared into the Sheik's quarters.

"Well, Anaya"—Copperhead's voice came smoothly through the system—*"your assets are being whittled away. Do you still want to do this the hard way?"*

Christal glanced up at the clock. "You bet, bitch."

Sid was hurrying down C Deck, testing doors as he went. But in the monitors, Christal could see ever-increasing numbers of security personnel trotting down the corridors.

It was just a matter of time.

CHAPTER 35

It could have been déjà vu with repetitious redundancy. Once they had hustled Sheela up to the Sheik's opulent quarters, Hank Abrams indicated that she take a seat on the ornate chaise longue. The Sheik stood at his coffee machine—while light from the large windows gleamed on his immaculate black silk suit. This time she could see his diamond cuff links as he worked the levers of the espresso machine.

"Black again, Ms. Marks?" he asked in his clipped English.

"Sure," she said warily, wishing her heart wasn't hammering against her ribs. "What's the matter? You missed my company?"

"A bit of a problem, actually," he answered. "Your people are causing a measure of distress."

He glanced at her, his flat black eyes unforgiving as stone. "It will be good for us in the long run, I think. Security has become a little lax over the last couple of years. Isolation creates the illusion of invulnerability. Your arrival, auspicious as it is, is indicative that those days are now passed. Where you now intrude, so too will a curious media, authors, private investigators, and a host of others. Not to mention several of our business rivals anxious to scoop one of our patents."

"I'm thrilled to be of service."

The coffee machine hissed as he filled a cup and placed it on a delicate saucer. Hank carried it across the thick carpet to her. The Sheik gave her the same smile the fat woman gives the turkey on the day before Thanksgiving. "Please, enjoy. You may not have much time."

Hank Abrams had stepped over by the door where Achmed stood at his post. Abrams had a radio to the side of his head, an intent expression on his face as he listened, and then talked.

He turned. "We've got Bridges, sir. Where would you like him?"

Sheela's heart leaped. It took all of her concentration to keep her expression under control. Lymon's wry smile and sparkling eyes teased from her memory. She was going to hate to hear his muttered, "I told you so's."

The Sheik narrowed an eye, glanced at her, and then said, "Bring him here. I want them all together in one place. I take it there has been no progress at the SC?"

Abrams might have been a battlefield lieutenant given his rod-stiff posture. "No, sir. Ms. Hayes is working on it. Apparently Anaya has the hatch secured some way."

Sheela straightened. *Christal!* So, she'd been here all along. The SC? What could that be? Sheela took a deep breath, pursing her lips as she took inventory of the ornate room. There had to be something here that she could use when the time came.

"The SC was designed to be secure against unauthorized entry," the Sheik said in a voice all the more ominous for its curious gentility. "How did she get past the hatch? Where did the error occur?"

"I don't know, sir. When this situation is under control, we'll make a very detailed analysis: how it developed—and how to ensure it doesn't happen again."

The Sheik's smile carried a predatory confidence. "I'm sure you will, Mr. Abrams. You seem quite adept at solving *past* problems."

Abrams's expression turned grim. "Yes, sir." He turned away, the radio to his ear. "Agent Hayes is currently bargaining with Anaya, sir. Do you have any specific instructions for her?"

The Sheik stepped over to stare down into Sheela's face. Marshaling all of her will, she lifted her eyebrow into an inquisitive arch.

"It's a fascinating strategic and tactical problem," Abdulla told her. "Your Ms. Anaya has some of my people, and I have some of hers. Don't you wish this was one of your movies? We would know how it ended, hmm?"

The door opened—breaking the war of wills—and blond-haired Neal led the party as Lymon was marched into the room. The grim expression on his face was one she'd never seen before: stressed, and clearly worried. Another of the security men, a flat-faced guy with a thick black beard, held an HK machine gun tight against Lymon's back. Sheela stood, her cup of coffee in hand. Thank God, he looked all right. When their eyes met, she couldn't help drawing a breath. A glittering desperation lay behind his eyes.

It was unlike him. What did he know that she didn't?

With a stiff hand, Neal shoved Lymon backward into one of the overstuffed chairs that lined the paneled wall. "If he gets out of that chair, Aziz, you shoot him, understand?"

Aziz jerked a quick nod and grinned as he hovered over Lymon's left shoulder, the HK's suppressor inches from Lymon's head.

Sheela knew that weapon, had handled it on the set of *Moon of Falling Leaves* several years before. Not exactly a box office flop, but not one of her stellar roles either; the picture had been about a housewife accidentally caught up in the drug trade. Yes, she knew the MP5. While prepping for the role, the weapons expert had given her a rundown on why it was the world's most successful submachine gun.

"Lymon?" she asked in a carefully modulated voice. "Are you all right?"

"Fine, Ms. Weaver."

"Cut the crap, asshole!" Neal Gray told him. "We know who she is, who you are, and who Sid Harness is, too."

"How about the White Rabbit?" Lymon asked. "You got him pegged, too?"

At a gesture from Neal, the guard pulled the heavy automatic weapon back and drove it hard, muzzle first, into the side of Lymon's head. Sheela heard the impact, saw Lymon's head snap sideways, and started forward.

"Stop that! Right now!" she commanded, her finger stabbing out like a knife.

The guard pulled the gun back, turning it so its black muzzle pointed at her. She felt her belly go hollow and crawly as the gaping bore centered on it.

"Enough!" the Sheik ordered as both Abrams and Gray stepped between Sheela and Lymon. Behind them she could see Lymon making a face, one eye squinting under the pain as his torn temple darkened with blood.

"You asshole!" She glared across Abrams' shoulder at Aziz, who stared emotionlessly in return.

Before anyone could react, Sheela lifted her little cup of coffee and dashed it over Gray's shoulder so that the hot liquid spattered on the guard's face.

Gray and Abrams rushed her, bearing her back to the fainting couch. After they'd flung her into the cushions, she got a glimpse of Lymon halfway to his feet, frozen as the gun-wielding Aziz glared at him over the sights. She could read rage in the Arab's bulging jaw as hot coffee dripped down his face and into his beard.

"I said, *enough*!" the Sheik barked. In a milder voice, he said, "You do like to take chances, Ms. Marks."

"You and your people," she told him as she gathered herself into a sitting posture, "are just digging yourselves in deeper."

The Sheik glanced at Lymon and snapped his fingers. "Attend to him. I don't want him bleeding all over the furniture."

Sheela could see the first stream of red leaking down from Lymon's temple and along the line of his jaw. He gave her the faintest shake of the head, as if warning her against any further foolishness.

She ground her teeth and turned her attention to the Sheik. "What do you want from me?"

He took the empty cup and saucer from her hands

and walked back to the big table in the middle of the room. "For the moment, I would like you to coax Ms. Anaya out of my security center." He shot her a long, evaluative look. "Would you do that?"

She stood again and crossed her arms defiantly. "Why the hell should I?"

"Let us say that by doing so, you will be fostering trust, yes?" He cocked his head, a spider's smile on his lips. "And, you must admit that just as I and my people are, as you say, 'digging ourselves in deeper,' so are you and yours."

"What's the trade?" she asked, narrowing her eyes as Abrams stepped out of the bathroom with a damp washcloth in his hand and started dabbing at Lymon's head.

The Sheik stared thoughtfully at her. "Your lives, Ms. Marks. The chance for you to go home and make movies. Even for Mr. Bridges to continue to work in your employ. You might actually have the opportunity to enjoy this relationship you have just begun. I hear it's been platonic until now."

How could he know that?

She stiffened, a flicker of anger glowing against the cold fear inside her. "My personal life is none of your business."

His fingers rolled her empty coffee cup back and forth on its saucer. "Your actions directly affect the value of your genotype. For instance, if you take up prostitution on Santa Monica Boulevard, you will destroy the market for your embryos."

"Then maybe you had just better let us go while I can still maintain my value."

The smile died on his lips. "That is indeed one

option. But, by doing so, I must have assurances that you and your people would not dedicate yourselves to impeding Genesis Athena. Can you promise that? Hmm?"

He read her defiant expression and laughed. "Ah, yes, that's what I thought. So, you see, when it comes to perceived value, other strategies might prove to be more effective. Perhaps if your bodies were found in a small rental yacht adrift off the Florida Keys? Shall we say, asphyxiated by an unfortunate leak from the exhaust system?"

Sheela searched his hard black eyes. He meant it! She hurried to say, "No more movies, that way. No future for your investment."

"That is correct. We would just have to make do with the Sheela Marks legend, and hope, as with Marilyn Monroe, that a death cult of fascination developed."

He gave a faint shrug. "Genesis Athena's marketing abilities are substantial, and in many ways, virtually untapped. Handled correctly, given just the right spin in the media, you might just be worth a great deal more to us dead than alive."

A cold rush went down her spine. "You'd never get away with it."

"No?" He chuckled softly as he worked the levers on his coffee machine and filled yet another of the cups. "I suppose I wouldn't have much chance of obtaining Manny de Clerk's DNA from a bit of his foreskin, either. And I'd never manage something as impossible as obtaining your menstrual tissue from the ladies' room at a crowded Hollywood gala."

"Let's cut the bullshit, shall we?" Lymon was

pressing the blood-soaked washcloth to his temple, keeping pressure on the wound. "Let's look at this as a business proposition, okay? Killing us involves a lot of risk and expense. Any way you cut it, it's complicated. Kill us now, and you have to move the bodies to the scene. If you decide to kill us there, you've got to transport us alive, and hope nothing goes wrong. As the complexity rises, so does the probability for a fuckup. Stupid small things can go wrong. Stuff you can't plan for. Some pump jockey might recognize one of your people when he's fueling the yacht, or you might have a flat tire at an inopportune time while transporting the bodies. Maybe the Coast Guard picks that moment to do a safety inspection. In the real world, shit happens. Why take the chance?"

"Yes, and?"

"You want our silence and cooperation," Lymon said with a slight shrug. Water from the washrag was mixing with his blood, sending pink ribbons down his neck. "We want to go back and take up our lives where we left off."

"How do I know you will do that?"

Lymon's smile was bitter. "Because you've won."

"Lymon!" Sheela cried. "What's the matter with you?"

He said in an offhanded manner, "Sheela, what's the point? The Sheik's outfit is big, well-funded, and superbly organized. You can't stop it, so you might as well make the best of it. Trust me on this."

Confused, she tried to understand. Was this really her Lymon? Or had that blow to the head taken something out of him? Rattled his brain? Perhaps given him a concussion or something?

“What do you have in mind?” Neal Gray asked.

Lymon broke eye contact with Sheela, giving a nonchalant shrug. “Say you ship Sheela, Sid, and Anaya back to the mainland and keep me for insurance? In the meantime, I’ll get on the phone to Rex Gerber, Sheela’s business agent, and tell him we’re buying into Genesis Athena. Say he sends you a check for maybe...two million? We put that in an escrow account under both of our names.”

Sheela stared, open-mouthed. “What the *hell* are you doing, Lymon?”

“It’s business,” he told her bluntly, then directed his remarks to Gray. “Sheela and the rest go back to living their lives. Sid writes up a negative 302—that’s the FBI’s brand of favorite paperwork—and everything’s back to normal.”

“Lymon, I *won’t* have anything to do with this!”

“Sure you will,” he answered, as if willing her to obey, “because I’ll stay here. If you guys break your agreement, the Sheik can do whatever he wants to with me and can withdraw the two million to boot.”

“No!” Sheela brazenly walked over to look down at him. She ignored the guard’s angry stare. Beads of coffee still gleamed in the guy’s beard. “I see what you’re doing. No, Lymon. You’re not buying my life with yours. We’ll do this together, whatever it is.”

“Touching,” Hank Abrams said, his radio still to his ear. “But it appears that our people have cornered Sid Harness. He was in one of the creches. They’re bringing him up now.”

Sheela could see Lymon’s expression tightening.

“Ah,” the Sheik said amiably, “it appears that the

only problem remaining is Anaya. Let's solve that, shall we?"

"How, sir?" Gray asked. "She's barricaded in."

"It seems that we have all of her people. Perhaps it is time to use them."

CHAPTER 36

"Mfffutt!" Vince called.

Christal rolled her chair back, turning to see him as he struggled against the tape. No way he was getting free. She shifted in her chair and returned her attention to the wall of monitors. In the big central screen, April waited calmly in the hallway, her radio to her ear. The four goons were standing around and giving the world brooding looks that promised violence and mayhem. It had been long and fretful minutes since she'd seen Sid Harness bundled into the Sheik's quarters.

Vince made a muffled sound again. Since nothing was happening outside, Christal stepped over, bent down, and ripped the tape from his mouth. He screamed at the mustache hairs that went with it.

"You got a problem?" she asked.

"God, that hurt!"

"Besides that?"

"I gotta go to the bathroom."

"Right." She slapped the tape back across his mouth. "Go ahead. I won't watch."

Before returning to her seat, she checked Gregor's tape and made sure he wasn't working anything loose. He stared up at her with pleading eyes.

"You okay?"

"Mffft!" The tape worked under his nose.

"You know, you and Vince have the same accent."

She slipped into her chair just as Lymon's face formed on one of the monitors. *"Christal? You there?"* His voice came over the speaker as he spoke into one of the radios.

"Here, boss. What's the situation?"

"We're putting the final touches on a deal."

"Let me guess. The Sheik and all his companions in sin deliver themselves to us in cuffs with signed confessions, right?"

"This isn't the time for your questionable humor." Lymon's eyes narrowed. *"I want you to get ready to leave the security center. You will proceed under guard to one of the hatches, where you and Sid and Sheela will be taken by boat back to the mainland. After that, you will take a charter flight back to LA."*

"And what happens to you?"

"I'm staying here for the time being."

"Hostage, eh?"

"Volunteer," he corrected.

She glanced up at the clock. "Sorry, sir. I can't do that."

"It's an order, Christal."

"Yes, sir. But, as of this moment, consider me to be fired. Or I resign. Whatever."

"Christal, I'm dead serious. I want you out of that control room."

She stared at his face, reading his desperation. The hair on one side of his head was mussed and damp. The flesh looked swollen, and if she wasn't mistaken, weren't those bloodstains on his collar?

She keyed the mic. "Lymon, you're speaking under duress. Since I'm no longer in your employ, I've got to make my own calls. I think you understand the stakes here."

"Christal, you've got to trust me. It's over. We've all come to an agreement. Everyone's happy with it, so I want you to leave the control center now." A pause. *"Christal? Christal? Can you hear me?"*

Hank Abrams stepped into view, moving Lymon to one side and taking the radio. *"Hey, Christal, what's happening?"*

She keyed the mic again. "Not a hell of a lot—which is how I like it. I was just sitting here watching Copperhead on one of the monitors. She and her goons are looking a little upset. You might want to come up and offer some comfort and consolation."

His eyebrows twitched in the familiar way they always did when she annoyed him. *"The time for banter is up. You know, we could get nasty about this, but Christal, you don't want to pay the price if we do."*

"Why's that?" She glanced up at the clock.

"Because it's real hard to live out the rest of your life remembering the look on Mr. Bridges' face when I put a bullet in his brain. That's going to weigh on you, Christal. It's going to fill your nightmares until the day you finally die."

He smiled into the camera. *"Take a moment. Think*

*about how it will be. For the rest of your life, you'll see it as I raise a gun to his head. That interminable instant will pass, and—*bang! *You'll replay that in your dreams, in all your waking moments. It will be your own private hell."*

"Go fuck yourself, Hank."

"You sure you want to play the hard-on when people's lives are at stake?"

She nodded, then glanced up at the clock. Something was wrong. It should have happened by now.

"Christal? You just going to let him die?"

She caught the faint whiff of something sweetly metallic and clamped a hand to her nose. Turning, she could see Vince's head lolled to the side, his eyes half-closed, chest rising and falling.

She leaped from the chair, lungs starting to burn, and found the open locker. Bending, she pulled out one of the gas masks, fumbled at the straps, and found the filter cartridges in separate containers in a box. Her heart was pounding, lungs sucking at the base of her throat as she ripped one of the cardboard boxes open and unscrewed the filter canister.

She got the round canister inserted, its neoprene seal tight, and screwed the canister closed.

God, help me! She fought the urge to take a deep breath, to expel the sour air in her lungs as she fumbled the thing over her head and tried to adjust the straps.

In desperation, she clasped the mask to her head and gasped, stumbling to her chair and flopping down. The mask had a rubbery smell. She blinked her eyes and tried to determine if her senses were impaired.

Yes, sleepy—she could feel it—and stood, walking slowly to and fro, slapping her arms to her sides, willing herself to stay alert.

In the monitors, Hank was talking, his expression filled with that earnestness she'd once associated with optimism. She shook her head, feeling the tendrils of lethargy at the edge of her mind.

Picking up the mic, she said, "Can you hear me?"

"Sure, Christal. You're muffled but audible," Hank replied. *"Now, did I make my point?"*

"Sorry, Hank." She smiled wryly behind the mask. "I was a little busy."

She could see April and her goons stepping back as a small acetylene welder was rolled into position by the door. "Hank? You'd better tell your sweetie, Copperhead, that I'll shoot Vince the second they put that torch against the hinges."

"What are you talking about?" Hank's face had turned serious again.

"I'm talking about shooting one of my hostages. You torch my door, I'll shoot Vince. You shoot Lymon, I'll shoot McEwan. *Que lastima.*"

He seemed to be thinking; then, with a smile, he lifted the radio. *"You and I just got crossways, Christal. It doesn't have to stay that way, you know. We used to be friends. I genuinely liked you. What's changed?"*

"Remember when they sacrificed my ass over the Gonzales case? Did I hear you say a word in that hearing? Huh? Anything to indicate that you were just as culpable as I was?"

"Yeah, I know." He glanced up, concentrating on the monitor. *"It was Marsha."*

"Give me a break! You couldn't act like a human being because of Marsha?" She could feel her thoughts starting to clear. Maybe she hadn't gotten nearly the dose that had laid Vince and Gregor out on the floor.

"Neal made some phone calls. Did you know that Marsha's firm represented several of Gonzales's accounts?"

She stopped short, frowning behind the mask. "No. I didn't. Why didn't you? She was your wife."

"She never told me her business."

"So, how'd she get the camera into the van?"

"Turns out she dropped by just before we arrived to go on shift. Said she was looking for me. Tom Paris let her in. When she left, she said not to say anything, that she'd be back later and wanted to surprise me. My guess is that Tom didn't think anything about it. Then, when the shit started to come down, he kept his mouth shut. Or she found a way to help him keep his mouth shut."

"Son of a bitch!"

"Yeah." She could hear the question in his voice. *"Good old Marsha. Fucked us all. You, me, even the Bureau. Hey, you know, when this is all over, we could go pay her a visit. Just you and me."* A pause. *"You ever think of that?"*

"Your playmate, April, might disapprove." Christal looked at the monitor where the hall gang—as she'd come to call them—waited with their cutting torch.

Christal watched as April lifted her radio and said, *"It's not working, Hank. It's been more than enough time. That change in her voice, it wasn't the gas."*

"Bingo! Five points to Copperhead." Christal glanced up at the clock, shaking her head. What the hell had gone wrong? "Whatever kind of shit you're pumping in here, you'd better hope it doesn't kill Gregor and Vince. I didn't put a mask on either of them."

She could see the irritation in Hank's eyes. *"Then I guess we're back to shooting Lymon, and after that, Sid's next."*

"You're not thinking, Hank. You shoot Lymon, I shoot Vince. You shoot Sid, I shoot Gregor. Then what? You going to shoot Sheela? Are you sure you want to run the stakes up that high?"

He stepped back, dragging Lymon into the picture. He lifted a stainless HK 40 that she recognized as Lymon's and placed it against Bridges' temple. His thumb flicked the control lever to the fire position. *"What's it going to be, Christal?"*

She pressed the key on the mic, saying, "Go fuck yourself, Hank." Then she closed her eyes, a miserable sense of failure and premonition crashing down on her soul. It was past time. They'd failed. The witches were going to win.

CHAPTER 37

Sheela stared in disbelief as Hank Abrams raised his gun to Lymon's battered head. Hank's expression was pinched, hollow-eyed, as if he himself couldn't believe what he was about to do.

Achmed held the camera as if it were a grail, his hands cupped about it to make sure it took in the whole image. He'd laid his MP5 on the table, ready to reach.

"It will be a shame to ruin that piece of carpet," the Sheik said from the side. "And please, back him up against the wall. That caliber bullet will probably blow the back of his skull out, and it will be easier to clean up if the wall stops most of it."

"No!" Sheela cried, starting forward. Aziz cut her off, his eyes promising something nasty. She could see blisters on his face where the coffee had scalded.

"For God's sake!" Sid said where they'd placed him in the corner. "Let me talk to Christal! I can reason with her."

Lymon suddenly smiled as he stared into the

camera and shouted, "Go for it, Christal! God bless you!"

"Inshallah!" the Sheik muttered. "Just *shoot* him! We'll clean up later."

Sheela bent down and sank her teeth into the hand that clasped her shoulder. As the guard howled and flung her aside, she barely noticed Neal Gray, a look of amazement on his face as he stared out through one of the large windows.

"What the hell?" Gray said, taking another step toward the glass.

Sheela scuttled back and fell, hearing Aziz roar as he grabbed for her.

"Kill him!" The Sheik took another step toward Hank Abrams and raised his fist. "Do it! Or do I have to do it for you?"

From the floor, Sheela reached out, crying, "No! Lymon! No!"

Sweat had started to bead on Abrams' face, and he slowly shook his head. His hand wavered, and he lowered the pistol. "No," he said. "Not me."

Sheik Abdulla uttered some terrible curse in Arabic and wrenched the pistol out of Hank's hand before thrusting him backward, out of the way.

He turned to the camera, eyes fierce and hot. *"You will get out of my control room, you bitch!"* He jammed the pistol against Lymon's swollen head.

"I'll do anything!" Sheela shouted, leaping to her feet. "Whatever it takes to—"

"Fuck!" Gray shouted. *"I don't fucking believe this!"*

In the brief instant before the room lurched sideways, Sheela would have sworn she heard a crumpling sound, felt a shiver. A low rumble could be heard. Then, as if scattered by the fist of God, people were reeling, things were falling, and shouts broke out.

Amid the clatter and crash of falling dishes, crystal, and breaking glass, Sheela scrambled for balance. Loud snaps, like breaking wood, split the air. The great table slid, folding up thick Persian carpet like crinoline. Huge and heavy, it came within inches of crushing her against the trembling wall. She would remember the crazy sight of Achmed hitting the wall headfirst to slump in the wreckage. The Sheik and Lymon staggered, slammed into the wood-paneled wall, and the pistol blasted thunder into the rumbling chaos.

Earthquake! The first thought caught in Sheela's recoiling mind. She struggled against the folds of carpet that had rolled around her. The table tilted sideways, and something heavy hammered her in the middle of the back.

She reached around, feeling cold steel.

CHAPTER 38

When the world canted and heaved, Lymon grabbed Sheik Abdulla, feet milling against the vibrating floor. Together they crashed into the wall; Lymon managed to raise an arm as they tottered. The pistol went off as he shoved the Sheik's gun hand up; then they fell, each twisting and struggling to find footing in the wadded carpet.

The pistol! Get the damned pistol!

Lymon drove his elbow into the Sheik's side, then again, and again, as the man howled. What the fuck had happened? One minute, he'd been staring right into Death's face, eternally proud of Christal's defiance. The next they were rolling around on the floor while a deafening rumble filled the air and the floor bucked up and down like a Humvee on a mountain two-track.

Abdulla's head rose inches from Lymon's as he tried to turn the pistol. Lymon pulled back and jerked forward, butting his forehead into Abdulla's face. He felt and heard the bones breaking in the man's nose.

"Asshole! I'm gonna kill you!" he howled as he got

one hand around Abdulla's throat. His other hand clamped on the flailing wrist below the gun hand.

The Sheik was muttering something in Arabic when Lymon's iron grip choked it off.

"What the fuck!" Hank Abrams was shouting as he picked himself up off the floor. "What the fuck happened here?"

"We're grounded!" Neal Gray screamed. "We're grounded on some damn beach!"

The Sheik hammered a knee into Lymon's crotch. He gasped, writhed, and felt Abdulla twist free long enough to gasp, "Help me!"

Lymon roared in rage, flopping his body onto the Sheik's. Another shot rang out as the man's hand reflexively pulled the trigger.

A harsh order sounded, and Lymon looked up to see the bearded Aziz, somehow on his feet in the wadded carpet, staring down over the sights of his HK MP5.

Lymon swallowed hard and nodded, letting the Sheik go.

The man flailed away from Lymon's grip and scuttled over Achmed's slumped body. In the process, he stuck his hand in the hot water seeping from the spilled espresso machine and shrieked.

Lymon rolled onto his side. The room was in shambles: shaken, not stirred. One of the marble columns was splintered, the ceiling hanging, and several of the smaller tables lay on their sides. Two of the large windows had shattered.

"Kill him!" Abdulla hissed, trying to hold the pistol and cradle his burned hand at the same time.

Lymon's nerves went cold as the guard smiled through his black beard—and flipped the safety off. A gleam filled Aziz's black eyes as the sound-suppressed muzzle centered on Lymon's chest.

The staccato burst was too loud. It almost broke his eardrums.

Couldn't have come from the suppressed MP5.

It took a moment for his brain to catch up with the vision, but the guard's sides were jumping frantically, his eyes impossibly wide, and bits of red were making haze in the air.

Aziz seemed to weave in the sudden silence; the heavy HK rolled out of his grasp as if in slow motion. Then his knees went. He collapsed straight down, then flopped sideways into his own gore.

In the voice that had stopped countless cinematic bad guys, Sheela Marks ordered, *"Don't even think it!"*

Lymon lifted his head to see Sheela wading out of the accordioned carpet. She held an MP5 in the finest SWAT team entry form. Her face was a mask of determination as she centered the sights on the Sheik.

"Please relieve Abdulla of that pistol." Without breaking her gaze, she asked, "Lymon? Are you all right?"

Getting to his feet, he gave her a panic-induced grin. "Yeah." And reached out to snag the pistol from Abdulla's hand. "Nice gun work. Where'd you learn that?"

"Weapons expert on the set of *Moon of Falling Leaves*. But this one shoots real bullets."

"Hey!" Sid roared as Neal Gray scrambled for the door. "One move and I take you apart myself."

Lymon tossed his pistol to Sid. "Keep an eye on him." To the stunned Sheik, he said, "Sorry, pal, but the party's over." He bent to slip the remaining MP5's sling from the dead Aziz's shoulder.

Then—adrenaline pumping with the postcombat jitters—he walked to Sheela, bent to kiss her lips, and said, "God, I love you."

She spared him a quick smile. "I love you, too." A slight frown. "But what the hell just happened here?"

Together, they made their way to the shattered windows. Through the spears of hanging glass he could see a long gleaming stretch of beach. Behind the littoral, an irregular line of trees was cloaked in green through which the afternoon sun shone. People were already appearing on the shore, looking small as they pointed. And yes, wasn't that a park ranger's four-wheel-drive truck flying down the sand, light bar winking?

"What the hell happened?" Sheela asked, her MP5 still covering the Sheik.

"I think we just landed in New Jersey," Lymon told her in an awed voice.

"I've never liked Jersey," Sid muttered as he stood up from checking the dead guard's body. "God, is my boss ever gonna give me shit over this."

CHAPTER 39

Christal sat quietly in the darkness and dangled the weight of the gas mask from one hand. She replayed that last instant over and over. Seeing the monitors going black, feeling the shudder and then the jolt. Her chair had thrown her against the control board, and the room had gone black in an instant.

Oddly, the last monitor to go had been the one that showed Copperhead and her four goons tumbling down the passageway floor like broken dolls. It was even better than giving the bitch three good solid belts to the stomach. Paybacks were hell.

Then a silent and eternal night had fallen.

The worst part had been the waiting. Was Lymon alive? Had the Sheik killed him?

She smiled grimly in the darkness and said, "Hank, you always were a wuss."

She'd seen it in his eyes as he held the gun to Lymon's head. So, he'd done the right thing, but had it been for the right reasons?

A groan came softly out of the darkness. "Shit!"

"Good morning, Gregor." She wondered if it was morning. Her universe might have been stopped in time, frozen like existence at the edge of a black hole.

"What the hell? Where am I?"

"Security center."

"Turn the fucking lights on. I can't see a thing."

"Power's cut." She made a mocking face in the darkness.

"God, they've gone to that extreme? How long have I been out?"

"I haven't the faintest idea. Hours."

He shuffled in the darkness. "How on earth could I have gone to sleep?"

"Gas. Anesthetic, I think. They pumped it into the ventilation. I barely got to the gas masks in time." She smiled wryly. "Be glad they didn't use anything lethal. You'd be dead, bucko."

"You won't win, you know. They'll starve you out in the end."

"Sorry, Greg—"

"Gregor," he insisted.

"—but you've already lost."

"What?"

"You slept through being slid across the floor." She leaned back in the darkness. "I don't know how the hell they're going to get this thing off the beach."

"What are you talking about? Beach?"

"Yeah, Brian and I decided on Sandy Hook."

"What? Where's that?"

"New Jersey. It sticks up like a thumb on the south side of New York Harbor. It's a national recreation area. We thought it was perfect."

"Oh, come now! Stop the bluff."

She chuckled at the sincerity in his voice. "Greg, you've got no idea. You're through, buddy. Coast Guard is probably swarming around like fleas out there even as we speak."

"Right, lass, and if that were indeed the case"—he let his brogue deepen—"ye'd not be sitting in here on yer hands in the dark."

"Got that right. Problem is, the hatch is jammed. I tried it. You can turn the wheel, but I think the dogs are bent."

"No way!"

"Way." She took a deep breath. "Air's gone stale, too. Ventilation's gone. I hear bangs and creaks every so often but not much else. This hole's pretty soundproof. I think it was an eternity ago I heard a clang on the door. God knows what that meant."

"Assuming you're not lying through yer teeth, you think they've forgotten us?"

"That's a possibility. They might have their hands full. It was quite a jolt when we beached. Brian would have had them throttle up just before we ran aground."

"And why would the captain have done that?"

"You remember that black case that sat on the table when you first got us in here?"

"Aye."

"Turns out it belonged to Lymon. It had a Heckler and Koch sub gun and some other equipment in it. Enough that the bridge crew didn't hesitate when Brian ordered them to set a new course." She paused. "I hope he didn't have to kill any of them."

"Ach, are you trying to tell me that Brian fucking

Everly had the guts to commandeer the bridge? And that nobody noticed?"

She resettled herself in the darkness. "So, who had time to notice? Neal Gray, Hank, and April were totally occupied trying to run Lymon and Sid down at the same time they were trying to pry me out of here. My only concern was the Sheik. He was the guy who had the windows, who might have been able to see what was happening and react in time to stop it."

She smiled in the dark. "But God bless Sheela, she played the role of a lifetime. Kept him occupied and didn't even know it."

"So, yer telling me that we're run aground in New Jersey, that you and Brian did this all on yer own?"

"*Claro que si.* That's the way it is."

"Bullshit!"

A slight moan came from behind Vince's tape. Christal wondered if he'd ever managed to relieve the pressure in his bladder. She sniffed but wasn't sure she'd recognize the odor of urine in the stuffy air. She might have already grown used to it.

"Why don't you pull this tape off me, and we'll both try to open the damn hatch?"

"Just lie there in the darkness and shut up."

"Go ahead. Be smug. In the end, I've had the best of you, Anaya. How will you choose, you sanctimonious bitch? Will you give it life or—"

The clang was so loud she jumped. "Shit!"

"Aye. Someone knows we're here."

A slight glow turned from dark to cherry, to light red, then faded.

"What's that?" Gregor asked.

"I think they're cutting the hinges, Greg."

A lower glow could barely be made out, and then it, too, faded. Metal on metal rang out; then a grinding sound came through the steel. A high-pitched whine ended with a drill poking through and being withdrawn.

Christal grinned when a thin voice thick with Australian accent called, "Anybody alive in there?"

"Nobody but us mice," she shouted back at the hole.

"Be clear of the hatch. It's going to fall inward when we pry it."

Christal stumbled across the dark floor, feeling for Gregor's and Vince's bodies. Then she shouted, "Clear!"

The grinding sounded, and a thin line of light widened as the heavy hatch leaned, then crashed inward.

Christal blinked in the white light as Brian's tall shape stepped in, followed by two gray-clad Guardsmen.

Christal grinned as she stepped into Brian's arms. "Hey, it's good to see you."

"Good to see you, too. You all right?"

"Couldn't be better." She turned to the Guardsmen, pointing. "Those two need to be cuffed and confined ASAP. The charges are conspiracy to commit kidnapping, attempted murder, breaking and entering, tax evasion, and any kind of violation of maritime law you want to throw at them."

Then she reached up and kissed Brian Everly firmly on the lips.

CHAPTER 40

TWO DAYS LATER

Sheela padded across the carpet in her corner suite at the Plaza. Through the windows, she could see the street below: Manhattan traffic starting and stopping, joggers making dots of color as they trotted along the winding paths visible through the trees in the park.

On television, CNN continued to document the evacuation of the *ZoeGen* as, by groups of ten, the frightened passengers were removed, loaded into vans, and hauled off to the INS detention center for processing.

The press was in the midst of an incredible feeding frenzy. Each story that emerged fed an ever-greater appetite.

"Information on Sheik Amud Abdulla continues to trickle in," the commentator said. *"Apparently, he has been a strong supporter of US policies in the Gulf playing a hand in the pacification and rebuilding of Iraq. He has been*

instrumental in helping to stabilize the Gulf during building tensions with Iran. Senior White House officials are hinting that the Sheik, despite the grounding of his ship, has been cooperative and forthcoming during this investigation."

Dot, looking harried, walked into the room. "God, you wouldn't believe it! How do they figure these things out?"

"What now?"

"Somehow, angels alone know how, GMA's producer has figured out that you were aboard the *ZoeGen.*" Dot cocked her head. "Do you want to do the interview?"

"Tell him yes, but later. After things have settled down." She waved at the TV. "Dot, anything I say is just going to complicate matters."

Dot gave her a thoughtful look. "You understand, don't you? You couldn't *buy* better publicity."

"Good, because right now, that's the *last* thing I'd spend money on."

The frown deepened on Dot's forehead. "Tony called. I know you said you didn't want to talk to anyone, but he's on pins and needles to speak with you. I have him and GMA holding."

Sheela made a face. "Right. Tell GMA that the next interview I do will be theirs, and I'll take Tony's call here."

She walked over, settled herself in a settee beside a half-drunk cup of tea, and lifted the receiver. "Hello, Tony."

"Hey, babe! Wow! Is this some story or what, huh? Listen. I've got Bruckheimer on the other line. We've been talking. You know, throwing some pitches around. He's hot

to do your story. You know, the whole thing! Like from the tampon incident to you traveling incognito to snoop out Genesis Athena. It's like, name your price, babe! You can produce, whatever. Just give the word!"

"I need to think about it, Tony."

"Hey, babe! It's okay. Still too close, huh? Take a day or two to let it sit and digest. This stuff just keeps growing like mold in the refrigerator. I been talking to Benny. He thinks we can cast Camila Morrone to play Christal, and maybe even Chris Hemsworth as Lymon. Wouldn't that be a rip?"

"Tony, take a break."

"It's cool, babe. We're already working on the script. You know, just things I know. We'll have a treatment ready by the time you land in LA."

She hung up, rubbing her eyes and trying to shake off the sense of premonition. "This is going to be a nightmare."

Dot was watching with neutral eyes. "You were the one who wanted to take a month off."

"Why the hell doesn't Lymon call?"

Dot smiled. "Listen, you're just lucky that Sid Harness managed to get you extricated from that mess. Lymon and Christal are going to have their hands full for days. They're giving statements to investigators, talking to lawyers, filling in details. Thank God you were smart enough to fly Felix out to look after them. And what about this dead guy?" Dot's face tightened. "Did you really shoot him?"

Sheela glanced up, her face like a mask. "Dot, I think you have things to do. And while you're about them, make sure that we have a plane ready the moment the government cuts our people loose."

"Yes, ma'am."

After Dot left, Sheela looked down, barely bending her right index finger. In her mind, she could feel the gun vibrating in her hands.

"A short burst," she whispered, remembering the weapons training she'd received in preparation for *Moon of the Falling Leaves.* "So short. But now, everything's eternally different."

On the TV, photos of Elvis Presley and Princess Diana were being overlaid atop the beaming faces of two little babies.

"Are these cloned children really created from Elvis Presley and Princess Diana of Wales? As of this report, we have no reaction from either the Spencer family or the Presley estate."

Sheela gasped, staring in disbelieving horror at the young woman's face on TV. Krissy was smiling into the camera, that crazy gleam in her eyes. *"Oh, yes,"* she was saying. *"I went to Genesis Athena months ago."*

The camera pulled back to show Krissy pressing her hands to a swelling abdomen. *"Mine's a Sheela Marks baby! And I want everyone to know that I'm going to love her...the same way I love Sheela Marks!"*

For a moment, time seemed to stop. Sheela pressed a hand to her mouth, stifling a scream. Then, in horror, she bolted from the room, Krissy's madly gleeful expression burned into her brain.

CHAPTER 41

BEVERLY HILLS—TWO MONTHS LATER

"*In the end, I've had the best of you, Anaya.*" Gregor's words echoed hollowly.

The cold rage had continued to grow. Christal considered that as she put the Tahoe in park and killed the ignition.

"Don't go there." Brian's words hung in her ears.

"Got to," she muttered, aware of the coiled rage that was growing like a cancer inside her.

"How will you choose, you sanctimonious bitch?"

She had been raised Catholic. In the old church where the *santos* stared down from the walls at the stations of the cross. Down deep in her bones, she believed in heaven and hell, in the consignment to flames of woe. The decision she now faced tore her soul in two. But the choice couldn't be made—not yet, not until she had placed her foot atop the serpent's head and heard him squeal.

"Will you give it life or...?"

Christal finally understood the choice Gregor had left her to make.

She stepped out of her car and walked down between the manicured hedges. Her heavy hiking boots looked peculiar against the brushed cement of the walk. The place was a sprawling angular mansion of white cement, soaring windows, and great views of the surrounding mountains that gave way to the city. In the hazy distance, through the smog, the brassy gleam of the Pacific under the afternoon sun could be seen.

What was the moral choice?

She hated herself for having to make a decision that her upbringing, even her legal education, left her so ill-prepared for. One way she was a murderer in the eyes of her church, the other, an accomplice in the propagation of sin. Or, if she went through with it, wouldn't it be a form of suicide?

It is me...and it is not.

But, who are you, Christal Anaya? What are you?

The anger, the injustice of it, deepened as Christal stepped up to the great black door sunk in the white stucco wall. With a slim brown finger, she rang the buzzer at the call box, then leaned down, announcing, "It's Christal."

"Cool, babe. Be there in a sec," Tony's voice answered.

She hung over the abyss, lost and alone, facing eternal damnation.

How did one atone? She could hear Grandmother's distant voice hissing at her from somewhere beyond the grave.

Within moments Tony opened the door and stepped back. He was in a square-cut white shirt and wearing long baggy shorts. He held a margarita in each hand, offering one to her as he sang, "Da-dah! Cheers, babe! Here's to you."

Then he was off, padding barefoot across the tiles. "Come on. I'm poolside, you know? It's a perfect day for it. You up for a dip?"

"I didn't bring a suit." She stopped long enough to pour the margarita into a potted plant.

"Don't need one here, babe. No close neighbors—not that they'd mind anyway."

His house was nice—the sort of thing that, as a child outside of Nambe, New Mexico, she'd have once considered to be straight out of a fairy tale. She followed him out onto the terraced poolside. A tall stone formation spouted water that flowed down a cascading waterfall to a sparkling turquoise pool. He'd been right—from where she stood, none of the neighboring places were visible.

"So, Tony, did you read the screen treatment that your writers put together on the Genesis Athena thing?"

He turned, smiling in the golden sunlight. "Yeah, dynamite, I tell you. Bruckheimer's flipped over it. I mean, like, Sheela's still feeling fidgety, but she'll give in the end. This thing's gonna blow the top right out of the box office. Do you understand? Babe, there ain't never been nothing like it before! Sheela playing herself, pulling up all that rich emotion." He glanced down at her empty glass. "Wow! Sucked it down already, huh? I'll get you another."

"No." She set the glass on one of the poolside tables. Smiling, she took off her jacket. "I'm here for something else, Tony." She let her voice soften and raised an eyebrow as her coat slipped off her fingers. "Didn't you say it was a perfect day for it?"

Tony grinned, set his own drink down, and in one fluid movement, slipped his baggy shorts off. "Yeah, it is. You know, I've been thinking. It would be way cool if you played yourself." He crossed his arms and started to pull his shirt over his head. "You've got chops! The part—"

Christal's booted foot caught him squarely in the dangling genitals. The force of the blow lifted him off the cement, spiking a pain up her leg in the process. He screamed, staggering, trying to grab himself through the folds of the confining shirt. She stepped in close and used an elbow to hammer the side of his head. As he shrieked and screamed, she went after him: kicking and punching. Then, grabbing his staggering form, she bodily threw him through the poolside window.

The shirt ripped, leaving him blinking and moaning in the midst of the broken shards of glass. He tucked his knees to his chest, arms up protectively as he gaped up from his lime green carpet. *"Don't hurt me!* Christal? What the fuck?"

She stood over him, hands knotting, as she glared down. "It wasn't until I read the script that I knew. It was you, asshole. All the time it was you! Shit, you had Sheela's schedule, knew her every move. I couldn't figure out how Hank and Neal found me. You gave them my address, you piece of shit! And you tipped them that Sheela was onto them—that *I* was onto them! The whole time, you were ratting us out."

"No!" He tried to stand, and she took the opportunity to land a kick under his jaw. At the impact, his head snapped back, and he collapsed onto the glass.

She could see little dabs of blood sopping into the carpet.

"It's in the treatment, Tony! The details of how I was kidnapped, flown across the country, and carried aboard the *ZoeGen*. How I was locked in a tiny little cabin in the secure part of the ship. Nobody knows that outside of the FBI, asshole."

He raised his hands in a pleading gesture. His eyes were unfocused, and blood was leaking out of the corner of his mouth. "Don't," he whispered. "Don't hurt me anymore! I'm sorry! I'm fucking sorry!"

In bitter rage, she hauled off and kicked him again. "You're a piece of shit, Tony. A filthy piece of stinking shit."

She turned, walked back to her jacket, and picked it up from the cement. As she started for the door, she looked down. "Nice place you have here." She paused. "By the way, I'm pregnant."

She was out the door and in her Tahoe before the shakes started. She made it halfway to the main road before she had to pull over and cry.

CHAPTER 42

A lazy surf rolled itself against the pure white sand. Lymon glanced out at the turquoise water and squinted from behind his sunglasses. In the distance he could just see the green mound of St. Kitts floating at the edge of the blue. The warm salty breeze ruffled his too-colorful flower-pattern shirt and teased his legs below his white cutoffs. Beside him, Sid walked barefoot, trousers rolled, head down, with his coat thrown over his shoulder. His white shirt was unbuttoned at the collar to betray his black thatch of chest hair. Lymon could see the sunlight gleaming on the incipient bald spot at the back of Sid's head.

"They still haven't found April Hayes. The best guess is that she passed herself off as a patient. Wherever she is, she's gone to ground until the dust clears."

"What's the point of hiding?" Lymon reached down and picked up a seashell before flinging it into the light surf. "Hank and Neal are already out on bail. The

Sheik's jetted off to Qatar, and they've almost refloated *ZoeGen* off the beach at Sandy Hook. Hayes could have just cooled her heels like the rest of them."

"That's what I came to tell you. It's been a fucking madhouse. I've been hauled into meetings with everyone from the White House to the attorney general and the secretary of state. I've been grilled up one side and down the other. If there was a way they could twist the story, they've tried it." He glanced at Lymon. "A lot of people are really pissed about this, Lymon."

"Good, their pal Abdulla shouldn't have been acting like a sultan. Slavery went out with the Ottoman Empire."

Sid's expression soured. "That's not why they're pissed."

"No?"

"Most of them are wishing it just hadn't happened. That Everly hadn't driven that ship aground. Sure, they're pissed at the Sheik for stealing his little clones, but they're more worried about what it will do to stability in the Gulf."

He paused. "Lymon, I want you to prepare yourself. My superiors are telling me in not-so-subtle ways that they're going to, and I quote, 'Try to minimize the damage.'"

"'Minimize the damage?'" Lymon growled. "You heard the reports. Abdulla has clones of over four hundred women in his palace back in Doha."

"They want it to go away. It's politics. He's a powerful man. I've been told over and over what a great friend he is to the United States." Sid made a face. "You seen TV recently?"

"No."

"It's one Genesis Athena ad after another. Little angelic-looking children talking about how Genesis Athena's medical miracles saved their lives." Sid rubbed the back of his neck. "The whole world knows what Genesis Athena is, what they do, and how they sell it. Hits on their website topped eighty million last week."

Lymon fixed his gaze on the turquoise water. "I heard yesterday that Neal Gray just sold book rights for two million, and Hank Abrams—"

Sid gave him a look from the corner of his eye. "He could have pulled that trigger, boss. No matter what, you can't forget that."

"No, I suppose not. I just hated to hear he's been booked on every cable channel on the planet." He reached down to pitch another shell.

"You talk to Brian Everly?"

"No. But his embassy just kicked him loose. I heard he flew to LA first thing."

Lymon paused. "Christal had an abortion yesterday. Said she wasn't sure what that would do to her immortal soul. She wasn't happy about it."

"No, I suppose not." Sid stomped a wave. "What's it called when you abort your own clone? Suicide?"

"Well, just keep your mouth shut when we get back to the villa, huh?"

"How is Sheela? She coming to grips with it?"

"I guess. Felix has filed a civil suit against Genesis Athena. During our conference call last night, he said that they're already offering a five million out-of-court settlement tied up with a billion strings."

"She gonna take it?"

"I dunno."

Sid glanced around. "You sure I shouldn't just take the ferry back to Basseterre?"

"Yeah. The place is big enough you'll probably get lost in it as it is. We won't be disturbed unless we want to be."

Sid's lips tried to smile but failed. "You know, the whole world's looking for you two."

"Yeah, and to date, they haven't found us." He chucked another shell. "We rode to Montana on the Beemer, then caught a charter from Billings to Miami to here."

"Word is that Sheela Marks is the most sought-after interview in the world." Sid kicked at the pristine sand. "Your boy, Tony, made sure of that. I hear he's having trouble eating."

"It'll be another couple of weeks before they take the wires out. He's declined to press charges."

"I also hear that the Sheik and his investors are very pleased with Sheela's profile right now, and the last thing they want to do is upset her. You might get more than that five million."

"I'll tell the Sheik what he can do with his profile." Lymon felt his jaw muscles tensing and the slow anger burning around his heart.

"Don't, Lymon. Let it lie. Trust me on this. Just love the lady. Hold her and support her any way she needs it."

"Yeah."

"One last thing before we head back. Claire hates DC."

"So, move her."

"Yeah, well, you still interested in having someone help you with the IRS paperwork? I've got to give them two weeks' notice but after that..."

"You might give June a call."

"Yeah, I know. I've heard from a reliable source at LBA that she runs the place."

CHAPTER 43

It looked like the same world, but it wasn't. It never would be. Sheela sat in the shade beside the row of soft green plants on the villa balcony. Beside her, a lemonade sweated condensation in the tropical breeze. The droplets trickled down to soak the envelope on which the glass rested. The words GENESIS ATHENA were barely legible as the ink ran. Inside, absorbing the moisture, lay the Sheik's last insult: an invoice for the balance due on her procedure.

Down the tree-covered slope, she could see Lymon, walking tall and confidently across the sand beside Sid Harness. Every once in a while, Lymon would bend and toss something into the surf.

He's alive because of me.

She took a deep breath, staring out over the turquoise Caribbean water.

Yes, he was alive.

She closed her eyes, remembering the easy and languid sex they'd shared that morning before Sid's arrival. She recalled how she'd run her fingers down his sides and felt him shudder at her touch.

She had to believe that everything balanced, that the life she had taken made her love Lymon with a greater intensity. That the part of herself that had died in that blast of automatic fire had been replaced by something more profound. Each breath that Lymon took, each pulsing beat of his heart, had been bought and paid for by her sacrifice.

She placed a hand on the form-fitting white sundress and pressed her abdomen. How could she comprehend the eight million sperm he had shot inside her? All those copies of Lymon's DNA churning about in a frenzy of futility. Even as she sat there, they exhausted themselves by the thousands, frantic flagellae ceasing to thrash in her warm fluid. Energy spent, they drifted, carried relentlessly away from their goal by her dark vaginal currents. Did they surrender themselves to oblivion knowing they were already too late? Did some subtle hormone warn them that her womb was already taken?

She closed her eyes, trying to imagine what it looked like: Round, slightly rough on the outside. She could imagine it resting there against the blood-rich lining of her uterus. It had already begun to siphon energy and nourishment from her body. The first pangs of nausea had made their presence known that morning.

She still had to tell Lymon. And what would he say? That she was crazy?

No, not Lymon. But perhaps she was crazy in her own curious and odd fashion.

After an agony of indecision, Christal had chosen abortion.

I can't blame her.

She stared longingly at the two men as they turned and began retracing their tracks on the deserted beach. Lymon was on his way back to her. No matter what, she wouldn't face this alone. The knowledge warmed her soul in a way she couldn't describe.

She had met her devils, slain them, and come out stronger for it. The future would come with its own antagonistic choices, hard questions, and difficult explanations. One by one, she would face them, deal with them. She would do it with a steel conviction...and damn the critics. Perhaps now, finally, Father could be proud of his little runaway.

She took a deep breath and pressed on the softness above her uterus, carried away by the mystery of how they had managed to do it so quickly.

She wondered if she even cared.

I am the Madonna, brought to prominence through immaculate conception. Will my daughter be divine? Or just another life? Will she share my soul or create her own? And, if she creates her own soul, does that mean that the spark of God glows in each of us?

So, what was a person? A collection of proteins and molecules in which a discrete soul would eventually find a home? A piece of herself to replace the part that had died in that machine gun burst?

God must be laughing.

IF YOU LIKE THIS, YOU MAY ALSO ENJOY: THE VISITANT

THE ANASAZI MYSTERIES BOOK ONE BY W. MICHEAL GEAR AND KATHLEEN O'NEAL GEAR

***New York Times* bestselling authors W. Michael Gear and Kathleen O'Neal Gear premiere a captivating new mystery series packed with ancient myth.**

Archaeologist Dusty Stewart finds himself diving into a chilling excavation of an ancient massacre site when the echoes of an eight-hundred-year-old mystery reverberate, leaving tantalizing clues in its wake. But Dusty's expertise is not enough to decode the brutality etched into the remains, and—in a twist of fate—his nemesis is summoned to aid in deciphering the cryptic puzzle.

When Dr. Maureen Cole arrives at the scene just as a formidable artifact surfaces—the basilisk, a symbol of witches and the hidden realm of duplicity—her task is to trace an ancient blood trail, a path laden with betrayal and madness. Drawing on her anthropological expertise, Maureen embarks on a quest to unveil the truth behind the heinous crime that has remained shrouded for centuries.

But the horrors of the past have a way of intertwining with the present.

Across time, in the shadowy expanse of Hillside Village, a primeval monster known as Two Hearts lurks, moving invisibly through the Katsinas' People and casting a sinister shadow. And when War Chief Browser discovers his wife's brutal murder at its hands, he vows to end the methodical killer's reign by any means necessary—and uncover its terrifying secret once and for all.

Can Dusty and Maureen piece together the puzzle before the malevolent forces that span centuries ensnare them?

AVAILABLE NOW

ABOUT THE AUTHOR

W. Michael Gear is a *New York Times, USA Today,* and international bestselling author of sixty novels. With close to eighteen million copies of his books in print worldwide, his work has been translated into twenty-nine languages.

Gear has been inducted into the Western Writers Hall of Fame and the Colorado Authors' Hall of Fame—as well as won the Owen Wister Award, the Golden Spur Award, and the International Book Award for both Science Fiction and Action Suspense Fiction. He is also the recipient of the Frank Waters Award for lifetime contributions to Western writing.

Gear's work, inspired by anthropology and archaeology, is multilayered and has been called compelling, insidiously realistic, and masterful. Currently, he lives in northwestern Wyoming with his award-winning wife and co-author, Kathleen O'Neal Gear, and a charming sheltie named, Jake.

Made in the USA
Las Vegas, NV
29 April 2024

89310807R00163